Swish

Also by Elena Delle Donne

Hoops
Elle of the Ball
Full-Court Press
Out of Bounds
Digging Deep

My Shot

HOOPS
Swish

5

Elena Delle Donne

Simon & Schuster Books for Young Readers
New York London Toronto Sydney New Delhi

SIMON & SCHUSTER BOOKS FOR YOUNG READERS
An imprint of Simon & Schuster Children's Publishing Division
1230 Avenue of the Americas, New York, New York 10020

SIMON & SCHUSTER BOOKS FOR YOUNG READERS
is a trademark of Simon & Schuster, Inc.
For information about special discounts for bulk purchases, please
contact Simon & Schuster Special Sales at 1-866-506-1949 or
business@simonandschuster.com.
The Simon & Schuster Speakers Bureau can bring authors to your
live event. For more information or to book an event, contact the
Simon & Schuster Speakers Bureau at 1-866-248-3049 or visit our
website at www.simonspeakers.com.
Jacket design by Laurent Linn
Interior design by Hilary Zarycky
The text for this book was set in Minister.
Manufactured in the United States of America
0220 FFG
First Edition
2 4 6 8 10 9 7 5 3 1
Library of Congress Cataloging-in-Publication Data
Names: Delle Donne, Elena, author.
Title: Swish / Elena Delle Donne.
Description: First edition. | New York : Simon & Schuster Books
for Young Readers, [2020] | Series: Hoops ; 5 | Summary: After
briefly playing on the volleyball team, twelve-year-old Elle rejoins
the basketball team, helps them reach the playoffs, and creates a
booster club to support girls' sports teams at school.
Identifiers: LCCN 2019013552 (print) | LCCN 2019017502
(eBook) |
ISBN 9781534441286 (hardcover) | ISBN 9781534441309
(eBook)
Subjects: | CYAC: Basketball—Fiction. | Clubs—Fiction. |
Friendship—Fiction. | Discrimination—Fiction. | Middle schools—
Fiction. | Schools—Fiction.
Classification: LCC PZ7.1.D4558 (eBook) | LCC PZ7.1.D4558
Sw 2020 (print) | DDC [Fic]—dc23
LC record available at https://lccn.loc.gov/2019013552

To my goddaughter, Gia,

and all the young ballers out there

Acknowledgments

I have a team of people that I would like to thank, and I fully recognize that I would not be where I am today without the support of my family and friends behind me.

Amanda, my wife and my best friend, you have given up and sacrificed so much to help me better my career (even being my off-season workout partner). Words cannot express how much you mean to me, and I am so excited that you are with me for life. We are a pretty unstoppable team.

Special thanks to my incredible parents, who have been with me since day one. Mom, thank you for being extremely honest, absolutely hilarious, and my ultimate role model for what strength looks like.

Dad, thank you for driving me all the way to Pennsylvania twice a week, attending every AAU tournament, and still traveling to lots of my WNBA games. You are my biggest fan.

To my older sister, Lizzie, thank you for helping me keep everything in perspective. You remind me that there is so much more to life, and that joys can come from anywhere—even something as simple as the wind or a perfectly cooked rib eye. You are the greatest gift to our family. And thanks to my big brother, Gene, for being able to make me laugh, especially through the lows, and for being my biggest cheerleader.

Wrigley, my greatest friend and Greatest Dane. Thanks for being my rock in Chicago and for attacking me with love every time I come home. Rasta, thanks for being the edge and sass in our home and for being the only one in our house who can keep Amanda in check.

Erin Kane and Alyssa Romano, thank you for helping me discover myself and for helping me find my voice. This wouldn't have happened without the greatest team behind me.

Thanks to my Octagon literary agent, Jennifer Keene, for all her great work on this project. Thanks to the all-stars at Simon & Schuster, including Liz Kossnar.

Thank you all.

I'm Back!

"Pepperoni is the only kind of pizza that matters," Dina was saying.

Natalie made a face. "Ew! What is pepperoni supposed to be, anyway? I mean, they're like weird spicy coins of unidentified greasy meat."

"And delicious!" Dina replied, taking an enormous bite of her pizza slice.

It was a typical post-game pizza lunch celebration at Spike's Pizza Joint for the Nighthawks, the girls' seventh-grade basketball team at Spring Meadow School. That morning, the team had won a game against the Cardinals. Everybody was laughing and talking, and Dina was eating more slices of pizza than looked humanly possible. There was only one problem.

I wasn't on the team anymore.

That had been my own choice. A few weeks ago, I'd decided to take a break from basketball. I'd been questioning whether I really loved the sport, or whether I felt I *had* to play. When you're six feet tall and twelve years old, everybody expects you to be a basketball star.

So I'd quit. I'd helped out the girls' volleyball team for a few games while one of their players was out with an injury. Some of the girls on the Nighthawks had understood, like my best friend, Avery. But a few others, like Natalie, Hannah, and Bianca, had been pretty upset with me for leaving in the middle of the season and joining another sport.

But the season wasn't over yet. The Nighthawks were just a few games from the playoffs. I had gone to their game today, and they'd played great and won. Lauren, the injured player on the volleyball team, was better, so they only needed me for one more game. After watching the Nighthawks play I'd decided: I wanted to rejoin the basketball team!

The problem was, I didn't know how my coach or my teammates were going to feel about that. I wasn't sure how to tell them, but I thought it might be easier to start with my friends first.

"Do you want me to tell everybody?" Avery whispered, leaning in to me. "This might be a good time."

I scanned the faces of my former teammates. Natalie and Hannah would probably be happy to hear that I was coming back, since they'd been angry that I'd left in the first place. Caroline was chill, Amanda was sweet, and Patrice, the coach's daughter, was quiet and nice. No problem there.

That left Dina, Tiff, and Bianca. Dina could be pretty hot-headed and unpredictable, so I wasn't sure what she would do. Tiff was cool with me, but loyal to Bianca.

And Bianca . . . she and I had had problems since the beginning of the season, when Coach made me center and moved her to shooting guard. I guess I was most nervous about her reaction, but before coming out for pizza she had talked to me and asked me to come back. And promised to stop calling me stupid names and criticizing me all the time.

I had to believe her if I wanted to come back to the team.

Just girl up and tell everybody! I coached myself. I took a deep breath and raised my voice.

"Hey, everybody!" I said, and everyone quieted down and looked at me. I could feel myself blushing. "I just wanted to say that . . . um . . . I've been thinking, and . . ."

"Elle is rejoining the team!" Avery shouted out happily, and I flashed her a grateful look.

To my relief, a cheer went up from the table. Even Bianca looked happy about it.

"I still have to ask Coach," I said. "But if she says yes, I'll be back."

Patrice grinned at me. "That is awesome, Elle!"

"We missed you," said Caroline.

"Welcome back, Elle," Hanna added.

Amanda looked at me, her freckled nose wrinkled

with concern. "Are you sure, Elle? You're not going to leave again, are you?"

From the tone of her voice, I couldn't tell if she was saying it because she cared, or if she was challenging me. I was a little bit surprised, because Amanda and I get along really well. I figured I was misreading her. She couldn't be annoyed with me, could she?

"No, I won't quit the team again," I said. "I promise."

Bianca smiled. "Just in time to help us get to the playoffs," she said.

Dina raised her soda bottle. "Cheers to Elle! Cheers to the playoffs!"

We all raised our beverages and clinked. I felt great and couldn't wait to get back on the basketball court!

My bubble started to deflate just a teeny bit when I broke the news to my family at dinner that night. The whole Deluca family was seated around the table, eating Dad's famous Sunday night spaghetti and meatballs. Dad, Mom, me, my brother,

Jim, and my sister, Beth. My dog, Zobe, sat next to me on the floor, watching jealously as we passed plates of food back and forth.

"So I've decided to rejoin the Nighthawks," I blurted out between bites of garlic bread.

"That's good news!" Dad said.

"I knew you would," Jim added.

Mom looked at me with concern. "Are you sure about this, Elle? Really sure?"

I nodded. "I don't regret quitting. I had some good reasons to. Volleyball was a lot of fun, and I loved the energy of that team. Everyone there is really supportive of one another, and I didn't stress out during the games. I think I figured out that when I relax, I can concentrate better on my game."

"So why not stick with volleyball?" Mom asked.

"Even though it was fun, I didn't love the game. The pace, the action, it's really different than basketball," I explained. "It made me realize how much I missed being on the court. And that I really *do* love basketball."

Dad nodded. "Well, you know, Elle, you were—"

I interrupted him. "Please do *not* say that I was born to play basketball. Everybody always says that, and that's one of the reasons why I quit. I don't want to feel like I *have* to play. I want to do it because I *want* to. And I do. I want to be back on the team."

"Well, if that's the case, then I'm glad Coach took you back," Mom said.

"Well, I haven't exactly asked her yet," I admitted.

Mom frowned. "Don't get your hopes up, then, Elle. She might not let you play again until next season," she said. "After all, your other teammates have been putting in a lot of work, and you haven't played in weeks."

"I think you're wrong, Mom," Jim interrupted. "A few weeks away from the court hasn't hurt Elle. Coach Ramirez loves to win. She'll take Elle back in a heartbeat."

I was starting to feel unsure of myself. After dinner, I pulled up a chair next to Beth's wheelchair. She can't see or hear, so we communicate using a special form of sign language. When I sat next to her she grabbed my hand and formed the symbol for *dog* into it. I laughed.

"I think Beth loves Zobe more than she loves me now," I said.

"She loves both of you," Mom assured me.

I called Zobe over to us and started scratching his head. "Don't worry, Zobe, I'm not jealous. You can't help being so lovable."

Zobe is a Great Dane, so he's a big dog, but he's as cuddly and sweet as one of those giant teddy bears you win on the boardwalk. Beth reached out with both arms to pet him, and he nuzzled right into her with his big snout. I joined her in petting Zobe, and soon his tail was wagging with doggy happiness.

Being with Beth always calmed me down. Tomorrow was Monday, and I planned to talk to Coach before basketball practice—and hopefully, she'd let me stay. I knew that asking Coach wasn't going to be easy, but it wasn't going to be terrible, either. Still, I had butterflies in my stomach thinking about tomorrow!

· · ·

The next morning, me and my other best friend, Blake, got a ride to Spring Meadow School with Jim, who's a senior. Spring Meadow is a small private school near Wilmington, Delaware. There are three buildings: One for K to fifth grade, one for middle school, and one for high school. Each grade has about fifty kids in it, so we all pretty much know one another.

I walked into the building with a duffel bag containing my basketball shoes and practice clothes tucked under my arm. I was taking a chance that Coach Ramirez would let me back on the team— but I wanted to show Coach that I was prepared and ready to go.

As I floated through the school day—taking a World History quiz, eating a turkey burger at lunch, trying to sculpt Zobe out of clay in art class—in the back of my mind, I was preparing the speech I was going to give to Coach.

When the final bell rang, I grabbed the duffel bag from my locker and bolted across the field to the high school building, where we practiced in the gym. I found Coach behind the desk in the athletic department office, looking all-business as usual in a yellow polo shirt without wrinkles, and not a dark brown hair out of place.

I knocked on the door, and she looked up.

"Coach, can I talk to you please?" I asked.

She didn't seem surprised to see me, which puzzled me, until I remember that I had told Patrice about my decision. She had probably told her mom that I wanted to come back. I didn't know if that was a good thing or a bad thing, but my palms started to sweat.

"Have a seat, Elle," she said.

I sat down and took a deep breath. "So, Coach, I've done a lot of thinking, and I really want to come back to the team."

"Patrice told me," she said, confirming my guess.

I waited for her to say more, but there was an awkward pause.

"I'm sorry for leaving the team before," I said. "I just needed to make sure that I really loved playing basketball. And now I know that I do. I just have one volleyball game left on Friday, but I'm ready to start basketball practice right now." I held up my duffel bag.

Coach leaned across the desk, focusing her dark eyes on me. "Here's the thing, Elle. I expect a one hundred percent commitment from all my players. When you quit, you showed me that you couldn't commit," she said.

My mouth felt dry. All I could do was nod. She wasn't going to let me rejoin!

"But, I also understand that you're at an age where you're trying to figure out who you are," Coach said. "That's tough for me to remember sometimes, but I get it. I believe that you do want to come back. But if I let you back on the team, how do I know that you won't quit again?"

"I won't!" I promised. "I really want to play. I . . . I needed to figure out if I loved basketball, or if I was just playing because people thought I should. But I missed it. I love it. I swear."

Coach sat back, frowning. "When you quit the first time, it was hard on morale. But from what Patrice tells me, the rest of the girls want you back," she said. "Unlike you, they've been putting in the time all season. I can't guarantee that I'll let you play until you've proven yourself."

I nodded.

"I'm willing to give you another chance, Elle," Coach said. "But it's not going to be easy. We're trying to get into the playoffs and I'm going to be pushing everyone very hard. Can you handle it?"

I wanted to shout, *Yes*, but I knew I needed to give her a more careful answer.

"I don't mind working hard on something I love," I said. "Playing with the volleyball team—we work hard, but everyone is really supportive of one another. It made me a better player. It really helped that even though we practiced hard, and wanted to win, it felt fun. And I . . . I want to play basketball no matter what, but it would be nice if it could maybe feel that way too."

Coach looked at me like she was going to say something, but she didn't. She walked over to a closet and pulled out a green-and-yellow Nighthawks basketball jersey and a pair of matching shorts.

"Here you go, Elle," she said. "Don't disappoint me."

I stood up and took the uniform from her. "I won't. I promise! Thank you!"

Then I turned to leave the room, and in my excitement I tripped over the chair I'd been sitting in—but I caught myself before I fell. Embarrassed, I rushed out into the hallway.

I felt like whooping and cheering, but I didn't want Coach to hear me. Instead, I took out my phone and texted my mom.

I'm back on the team! I typed. *Pick me up after practice!*

Great news, Elle! Mom replied. *Have fun!*

Have fun. I stared at the words on the screen. That was the one thing I knew I had to remember. I knew I had something to prove to Coach, and to all my teammates—that I deserved to come back. I had to prove that I wasn't going to disappoint them again.

That was a lot of pressure. But I knew that if I played basketball because it was fun, and because I loved it, everything would work out fine.

"Pretty Good, for a Girls' Team"

E lle's back!" Natalie shouted as I entered the locker room.

"Does this mean Mom said that you can join the team?" Patrice asked.

I grinned. "She did," I said. "Thanks for talking to her."

Patrice walked up to me. "You did the same for me. I feel so much better now, and it's all because of you."

"I didn't really do much," I said.

Patrice had been feeling really sore and kept

getting headaches. She was afraid her mom would think she was just trying to get out of playing basketball, so she didn't tell her. But I was worried about Patrice, so I talked to my mom, and Mom talked to Coach Ramirez.

Coach wasn't mad at all. She took Patrice for some tests and it turned out she had early-stage Lyme disease—that disease you can get when you get bitten by a tick. Patrice has to take medication, but says she has a lot more energy already. In the game on Sunday, she'd played better than I'd ever seen her.

I quickly changed into my practice clothes and then put on the new basketball shoes that my aunt and uncle had gotten me for Christmas. They were black with green stripes to match the uniform. They had great cushion and bounce, and I couldn't wait to play in them. Basketball shoes are one of the reasons I love the sport. Sometimes when I'm daydreaming, I imagine being a pro player with my own line of shoes. The only trouble is, I can never think of the right name. Air Delucas didn't have a ring to it. Electric Elle? That was terrible, but I knew I'd have plenty of time to think of a name.

I laced up my new shoes and joined the team in the gym. Coach didn't even address the fact that I was back on the team, which was maybe a little weird, but also it made me feel like I had never left, which was good. As always, she started by showing video of Sunday's game, fast-forwarding and stopping when she wanted to point something out.

"All in all, that was a great game on Sunday," Coach finished up. "I think we need to be stronger on defense, though. So after we warm up we're going to do some defensive drills. First, everybody up! Give me ten laps!"

We ran ten laps around the gym, and seeing all my basketball teammates in a row filled me with a happy feeling. Then we stretched, and did some exercises, and then Coach called us onto the court.

"I watched some videos by college coaches to get some defensive drill ideas," she said. "Let's start with one that looks like a lot of fun."

Fun? I don't think I'd ever heard Coach use that

word before. I wondered if what I'd said before practice had made a difference.

Coach grabbed a basketball and moved to the shooting line. "All right, I need you to line up in two lines across the court in front of me, with your backs to the basket."

We all quickly obeyed. I ended up in the second row.

Coach tucked the ball under her arm and clapped twice. "Defense!" she shouted.

Instinctively, we all shouted back, "Defense!"

"Let me hear you!" Coach cried. She clapped twice again. "Defense!"

"DEFENSE!"

"Better!" she said. "Now, when I yell 'Stance!' I want you to get into a defensive stance. Knees apart. Slightly bent. Reach down and touch the floor. Got it?"

"Yes, Coach!" We sounded like a troop of military recruits.

She clapped twice. "Defense!"

"DEFENSE!"

"Stance!"

We all touched the floor.

"Stance!"

We did it again.

Coach held the ball in two hands. "Okay, now you all are guarding me. When I move the ball, I want you to move your arms like you're shadowing that ball. So when I move to the right . . ."

She moved the ball to the right side of her body. We all moved our arms like we were guarding her.

"Good!" she yelled. She moved the ball to the left side of her body, and we moved to guard her. Then she raised the ball above her head, and we all raised our arms.

"Okay, let's add some movement," Coach continued. "Whenever you move to guard me, move a few steps right, left, or forward."

She held the ball out to the right again.

"Defense!"

"DEFENSE!"

"Defense!"

"DEFENSE!"

My heart was pumping. I was yelling really

loudly. I was moving my body. And I was having fun!

Coach continued the drill until we were all sweating. Then she taught us another drill.

Me and Bianca stood at the three-point line, each of us holding a ball. Four girls lined up in front of me, one behind the other, and four girls lined up in front of Bianca. When Coach blew her whistle, Bianca and I moved like we were going to shoot. The first girl on each line ran up to us. In my case, it was Amanda, and Dina ran up to Bianca.

"Block the shot!" Coach yelled, and Amanda and Dina jumped up, trying to block it. Then Coach blew her whistle again, and Amanda and Dina ran to the back of their lines, and the next two girls ran up. I liked how fast-paced it was!

Coach kept the drill going until the defenders had tried to guard us several times. Then she made Avery and Tiff the shooters so that Bianca and I had a chance to defend.

When the second drill ended, we were all pumped up with energy. Coach divided us into two teams for a scrimmage, like she usually does at practice. I ended up on a team with Avery, Dina, Patrice, and Amanda.

"Okay, centers, tip off!" Coach called out.

Bianca ran to the center of the court for her team, and so did I. But also, so did Amanda! I remembered that when I quit the team, Coach had made Amanda the backup center.

There was an awkward moment as we both stood there. To end it, I jogged past Amanda and motioned for her to take the position. She smiled at me.

Then Coach called out, "Elle, why don't you play center for this scrimmage?"

"I'm sorry," I said to Amanda.

She tossed the ball back to me. "It's okay," she said, but she wasn't smiling anymore.

I felt awful, but I shook off the feeling. Even though it was just a practice scrimmage, I felt like Coach was testing me. I had to show her that she hadn't made a mistake, and that I should be the team's starting center again.

Coach tossed the ball between me and Bianca, and I shot up like a rocket and batted it to Dina. Then I charged down the court. Dina passed it to

Avery, who shot a layup that bounced off the backboard. I grabbed it out of the air and then sank a clean shot. *Swish!*

Avery grinned. "Nice one, Elle!"

I felt like cheering as I ran back down the court. I was back, and it felt great!

Our team won the scrimmage by three points. Before we got changed, Coach made an announcement.

"I'm sorry, but I need to cancel practice on Wednesday," she said. "We'll have a regular practice on Friday. I will see you then."

Practice on Friday! I still had one more volleyball game to play on Friday night, and we usually practiced beforehand. I was going to ask Coach if I could miss Friday's practice, but I had a feeling that wasn't a good idea.

On the way to the locker room, she tapped me on the shoulder. "Good effort out there today, Elle!"

"Thanks," I said, and I waited for her to tell me that I was going to be starting center again, but she didn't say anything more.

I knew I definitely couldn't miss Friday's practice now. I'd have to work out something with the volleyball team. But I was kind of glad we had no practice on Wednesday. That meant that I could go to another meeting of the Buddy Club, which I thought I might have to quit because of basketball practice. I really didn't want to leave the Buddy Club, but at least now I could explain things to everybody and see if there were still things I could do to help, even if I had to miss meetings for a couple more months.

After we changed, we marched back across the field to be picked up by our rides. Dina started clapping.

"Defense!"

"DEFENSE!" we shouted back.

Some kids gave us weird looks, but we didn't care. We were still riding a high from practice, and I kept chanting as I climbed into the car with Mom.

"It sounds like practice went well," Mom said.

"It did," I said. "DEFENSE!"

When we got home, I quickly took Zobe for a short walk before I showered and changed. Mom didn't like me walking him in the dark, and I only had about thirty minutes before the sunset turned into a black sky.

As I neared the park, I saw that Amanda was doing the same thing with her dog, Freckles. She lives across the street from the park and I bump into her there a lot. And sometimes we make plans to meet at the dog park for "Doggy Dates."

I always get a little fluttery feeling in my stomach when I run into Amanda. I didn't know her too well before this year, because it was her first year playing basketball. She's really nice and funny, and we both love dogs. And when she smiles at you, it's like sunshine on a cold day.

"Amanda!" I called out, and I ran toward her with Zobe.

"Oh, hey," she said. She seemed distracted.

"I'm sorry about, you know, Coach putting me in as center for the scrimmage," I stammered. I still felt bad about that. "I don't know what will happen at the game. I mean, I know you put in a lot of hard work at that position and everything."

"Whatever. It's cool," she replied. "Look, I have to get home. Dinner."

"Okay," I said. I leaned over and patted Freckles on the head. "Bye, Freckles!"

Freckles, an English springer spaniel with long, droopy ears, gave me a big wet kiss on the cheek with her pink tongue.

Amanda laughed, and it was a relief to see her smile again. "See you tomorrow, Elle."

"See you!" I said, and then I slapped Zobe on the butt. "Come on, boy, let's run home!"

When I got home, Zobe and I bounded through the front door.

"Whoa!" Mom said. "Why don't you shower and use some of that energy to help me get dinner ready?"

"Sure," I said, and I moved to head up to my room, but then I stopped. Mom had the local news on the kitchen TV, and an image of a high school girls' basketball game flashed on the scene.

Any time I see women playing basketball, I'm instantly transfixed.

"One minute, Mom," I said, and I sat down to watch.

A guy sports reporter was talking to the camera. "We're seeing some exciting things happening in the Wilmington girls' basketball scene," he was saying. "Bethany Rodgers from Becker Heights is poised to break the state scoring record this season."

"Yes, she is quite a talent," said the female news-caster sitting next to him. "The Bobcats are having a great season this year."

The sports guy nodded. "They're pretty good, for a girls' team."

Mom stopped chopping carrots and looked at me.

"Did you hear that?" she asked.

I nodded. "What does that mean, they're pretty good *for a girls' team*?"

"It means that Rob Robertson of Channel 12 News has rocks in his head," Mom said, and she sounded angry. "No, I didn't mean that. But he's clearly misguided."

"Yeah. He makes it seems like girls' teams nor-mally aren't that good," I said.

"He's not the only one who does that," Mom continued. "It's like when people say Serena Williams is a great female tennis player. She's a great *tennis player*! Think about it, Elle. They never say that Tiger Woods is a great *male* golf player. They just say he's a golf player."

Mom was kind of blowing my mind. I mean, I guess I had been aware of this stuff, but it had never bothered me before. But Mom was clearly bothered.

"You seem upset," I said.

"Well, I am," Mom replied. "You and your brother both excel at sports. It's possible that you might want to pursue sports professionally one day. But the fact is that there are more opportunities for your brother to succeed in sports than for you. And I just don't think that's fair."

"I guess it's not," I said. "But maybe it will change by the time I'm old enough to go pro."

"It will only change if people fight for it," Mom said. "Right after dinner, I'm going to e-mail that TV station and ask for Rob Robertson to retract his comments."

"Way to go, Mom!" I cried. I high-fived her, and she laughed.

"Now please take a shower, Elle," she said. "I could use some help with the salad."

"You got it!" I said, and I ran upstairs.

In the shower, as the hot water hit me, I started to think about what Mom had said. She was right, about how women sports stars got different respect than male sports stars. From my basketball shoe obsession, I knew that currently thirteen male basketball players had their own shoe lines, and it was almost impossible to find a WNBA basketball player with her own shoe line. That definitely didn't seem fair.

It's not fair, but what can you do about it? a voice in my head asked me. It was nice that Mom was e-mailing the TV station, but would that help?

Maybe it would, and maybe it wouldn't. There was plenty of time for things to change. I was twelve years old.

Right now, I was ravenous from practice. All I wanted to think about was dinner!

Have a Heart!

"This is going to be the last time I can come to a Buddy Club meeting until basketball season is over," I told the group, as I took my seat for the meeting after school on Wednesday. "I still want to be a part of it, though."

"Of course you are welcome to stay in the group, Elle," said Ms. Ebear. "Not everything we do will happen at a Wednesday meeting, either."

"Thanks," I said, and I leaned back, relieved. I hated the idea of leaving the Buddy Club.

The club had been Ms. Ebear's idea. Not only

is she my World History teacher, but she's the best teacher I've ever had. When she teaches it's like she's telling a story, and she makes every lesson interesting. She's also really nice and a good listener.

At the first meeting, there had just been five of us in the group: Cole, the eighth-grade president; Dylan, who's in my grade; and Gabrielle and Katie from sixth grade. Today, there were three more of us.

Mrs. Ebear had us go around in a circle and introduce ourselves.

"I'm Satoko," said the girl sitting next to Katie. "I'm in sixth grade."

"I'm Emily, and I'm in eighth grade with Faith," said a girl with long blond hair.

"Hey, you did both of us!" Faith said, and Emily laughed.

"Sorry," Emily said.

"Thanks for coming," Ms. Ebear said. "Does anyone want to tell Satoko, Emily, and Faith what we've been doing?"

Cole raised his hand. "We've been discussing what it means to be bullied. We have been reaching out to kids we know who don't have many friends. And at the last meeting, I proposed that we come up with a strategy for an anti-bullying campaign."

To me, Cole sounded like a politician when he talked. He never stammered or blushed or looked uncomfortable. And he had an answer for every-thing, which was pretty impressive, I guess.

Katie held up a poster she had made. On a blue background with fluffy white clouds and a sun, were big bubble letters: BE A BUDDY, NOT A BULLY!

"I saw this online," she said shyly.

"I like that," I said. "It has the word 'buddy' in it, like the Buddy Club."

Katie smiled at me.

Cole started flipping through the screen of a com-puter tablet. "Posters are part of my threefold action plan," he said. "The other parts are an article in the school paper, and announcements during home-room."

Ms. Ebear got up and started writing on the board. "Okay, let's write down everyone's ideas and then discuss them."

Emily raised her hand. "I wanted to talk about the upcoming Valentine's Day Dance," she said.

I groaned. One thing about going to a private school is that they have a lot of traditional events. In the fall, they have this mandatory thing called a cotillion where you have to do a formal dance in front of everybody. They used to force girls to wear fancy dresses, too, but Mom helped get that rule changed after I freaked out because I hate wearing dresses.

Also, there's no more rule that random boys and girls are paired up to dance. Now you can dance with a friend, whether it's a boy or girl. Before the rule changed, I got paired with Dylan. It was okay because he's nice, but also awkward because he's about a foot shorter than I am.

"Why does this school love dances so much?" I wondered out loud, and Dylan laughed.

"That's what I want to talk about," Emily said. "I don't know if it's bullying, exactly, but I know kids get left out a lot at dances. Like, maybe they have nobody to hang out with. Or sometimes they get made fun of for what they're wearing."

Ms. Ebear nodded. "School functions can be awkward and problematic," she said. "But they're also a good opportunity for students to learn skills that will help them in the real world."

"Like dancing?" I asked.

"Not dancing, but social skills," Ms. Ebear said. She wrote *Valentine's Day Dance* on the board. "I'm intrigued by this, Emily. I think there's something not quite right about having a dance celebrating a romantic holiday for kids in middle school."

"Yeah, why does it have to be romantic?" Gabrielle wondered. "Why can't it just be about, you know, friends? Like a Friendship Dance?"

Katie clapped her hands. "Ooh, a Buddy Dance!"

"I like that idea," Cole said. "The eighth-grade student council is organizing the dance. Maybe we could ask them if the Buddy Club could sponsor it. We could change it to a Friendship Dance or a Buddy Dance and really get our message across."

Faith frowned. "But how would we decorate a Friendship Dance? Could we still use hearts and stuff?"

"Those hearts always have the dumbest sayings," Dylan complained.

Satoko spoke up. "I know! Like 'Kiss me' and 'You're hot.' Gross!"

"Definitely not appropriate," Ms. Ebear agreed.

"But hearts are so cute!" Gabrielle said. "We have to have hearts!"

I had an idea. "Maybe it's not hearts that are the problem," I said. "Maybe we could think of better sayings for the hearts. Like the one on Katie's poster."

Katie squealed. "Ooh, there are lots of good anti-bully sayings online! That's a great idea."

"Wait, wait," Emily said. "Maybe we can do more than just make those hearts for the party."

"What do you mean?" Faith asked.

"You know how people leave affirmation notes on bathroom mirrors and stuff?" she asked.

"Like, 'You matter' and 'You are beautiful,'" Ms. Ebear said.

"Exactly!" Emily said. "Well, why don't we make affirmation hearts for everybody in the school? We can put one on every locker the week of the dance."

"We can do it at night, so it will be a surprise," Katie said.

Cole nodded. "That would be a really effective way of getting our message across. Everyone would be talking about the Buddy Club." He looked at Emily. "How come you've never run for student council? You'd be great!"

Emily smiled at him and blushed a little.

Oh boy, I thought. *Are Cole and Emily making a crush connection in Buddy Club?* I couldn't decide if that was awkward or cute.

Ms. Ebear wrote *Locker Affirmations* on the board. "I think we've come up with some great ideas. What does everybody think?"

"I think that if we take over the dance, and do the lockers, that will be more effective than my original plan," Cole said. He looked at Katie. "Although I did like your poster, Katie."

"That's okay," she said. "I think making all those hearts is going to be fun."

"We've got a lot of hearts to make," Ms. Ebear

said. "We can work on them during our Wednesday meetings, but we might need to come in on a Saturday."

"I can come on a Saturday," I offered.

"Can we bring friends to help?" Satoko asked.

"The more the merrier," Ms. Ebear said. "Let's go over some goal dates. We've only got a few weeks until the dance. And Cole, I assume you'll talk to the student council?"

"On it!" Cole said, as he typed into his phone.

Ms. Ebear grinned at us. "You know what I loved about this meeting? Everybody had something to contribute. It just goes to show that good things happen when people work together."

"Like a team," Dylan said. And then he added, a little bit awkwardly, "Elle would know, right? From the basketball team?"

"Uh, yeah," I said. "Teamwork is really important when you play a sport."

Dylan was still looking at me, and I had an alarming thought: *Was* he *trying to make a crush connection with* me? I hoped not, because while Dylan is a very nice person, I have zero interest in dating boys. Zero.

Maybe all this Valentine's Day talk is making every-one crazy, I thought. *I'm glad we're changing it to Buddy Day!*

The Big, Bad Wolves

The rest of that week was a blur. On Thursday, I caught up on my homework. Then on Friday, I went to basketball practice instead of volleyball practice—Coach Patel, the volleyball coach, totally understood my dilemma. After basketball practice, Mom drove me to my last volleyball game.

My teammate Jenna put both hands over her heart when I walked into the gym at Harrison Prep.

"I can't take it! Elle's last game!" she said dramatically.

"Are you sure we can't convince you to stay?"

asked Summer, flashing a smile of perfect white teeth. With her golden blond hair, she looked just like her name.

"My heart belongs to basketball," I told them. "But I've had a total blast playing with you guys."

"You still owe us one more game!" said Kenya, the team captain. "Don't let us down, Elle!"

"I won't," I promised, and I didn't. Three of my serves earned us direct points, and I spiked two balls over the net to score. Not bad! We handily beat Harrison, winning the first two games in the best-of-three match.

"We're going to miss our Ace," Kenya said. (The team had nicknamed me Ace because of my killer serves.)

"Come out to celebrate with us!" Jenna pleaded.

I turned them down, because it was 9:30, and I was beat. Besides, I didn't want to be wrecked for Sunday's game. On Saturday I laid pretty low. Dad and I took Zobe to obedience class in the morning, and in the afternoon, I headed out into the chilly November air for a driveway game of pickup with Blake.

Blake has lived next door to me our whole lives, and playing basketball is how we became good friends. Well, it's one way we became good friends. We have also bonded over video games, superhero movies, and the awesome playground in the park.

"Oh yeah? You've had like, what, two practices?" he teased, dribbling the ball around me.

"Two practices *this week*," I said. "I wasn't even away from the team that long. I've still got it." To prove it, I stole the ball from him.

"Hey!" he yelled, as I dribbled to the basket for a quick layup. "I was just kidding!"

"Yeah, I know," I said, and I sank down on the curb of the driveway and gulped down some icy cold water from my bottle. Blake sat next to me.

"Bianca's really glad you're back," he said.

"Yeah, she's been cool," I told him. Blake and Bianca were sort of dating, although Blake's mom had no idea so I'm not really sure if it counted.

"You came back just in time for the game against the Wolves," Blake said.

I nodded. It had been years since any team from

Spring Meadow had beaten the Wallton Wolves. Playing them was always a lot of pressure.

"We've got our game against the Wolves right after yours," Blake said. "Bianca and Tiff are going to stay and see it."

"I'll stay too!" I said. "Most of the time, I can't get to your games because of *our* games."

"Well, now you can," Blake said. He stood up and took the ball from me. "After you guys beat the Wolves, you can watch *us* beat the Wolves!"

He sank the ball into the net to make his point, and I laughed.

"I'm not afraid of any big bad wolves!" I said.

But Sunday afternoon, running out onto the high school court in my Nighthawks uniform, nervous energy was racing through my body.

"Nighthawks, shooting drill!" Coach Ramirez yelled.

I lined up behind the three-point line with my teammates and took turns shooting. I made my first shot and as I ran back to the end of the line, I glanced at the mostly empty stands. Not too many students came to our games. But a bunch of Spring Meadow parents were there, including mine, wearing green and yellow. Caroline's little brother, Pete, was there, cheering me on like he always does.

"It's Elle! Elle is playing again!" he was calling out, and I waved to him.

"Hey, Pete!"

Caroline looked at me and laughed. I'd met Pete when I started volunteering for Camp Cooperation, the after-school program for kids with special needs. I thought Pete was adorable, and he'd become my biggest fan. Caroline could have been jealous, but she thought it was cute.

There were three people there who I wasn't expecting to see: Kenya, Summer, and Jenna from the volleyball team. I waved to them, and they waved back.

"Go, Elle!" Jenna yelled, and I grinned. Had they come to the game just to see me?

After our shooting drill, Coach called us off the court.

"Is everybody ready for today's game?" she asked.

"Yes, Coach!" we all shouted.

Dina looked over at the Wolves in their brown-and-red uniforms.

"They don't look so scary. Elle's taller than all of them," she said, and she was right. "Why does every-body keep talking about a curse or something?"

"Yeah, they say it's impossible for the Night-hawks to beat them," Natalie said.

Coach Ramirez frowned. "I don't want to hear any superstitious talk from you guys, got it?" she said. "They are a strong, solid team, but they're not magic. It doesn't matter how many games they've won, or who they've beaten. The scale can change its balance at any time. Today is our chance to beat them, and we will. Isn't that right?"

"YES, COACH!" we replied.

Then we made a circle and put our hands together. "Go, Nighthawks!" we cheered.

The ref's whistle blew.

"Elle, Bianca, Avery, Tiff, Dina!" Coach called out, and the five of us ran out onto the court. I noticed that Coach had put in our five best players to start, which maybe meant that she was more nervous about the Wolves than she was letting on. But I couldn't focus on that.

I faced off against the Wolves center, who was about six inches shorter than me. When the ref tossed up the ball, I easily outreached her and tipped it to Avery. Avery dribbled a few feet and then passed it back to me. I dribbled down to the basket with my back to the defenders. But when I stopped to shoot, three Wolves defenders surrounded me in a tight circle. I couldn't get my arms up for the shot.

Tweet! "Three seconds!" the ref shouted.

I had broken the three-second rule! I tossed the ball to the ref and she gave it to the Wolves to throw it in.

That wasn't how I had wanted to start the game, but I was confused. I had seen that type of defense in the pros before. It's called double-teaming or crowding when you let more than one defender cover a shooter. For some reason, I didn't think it was legal play in the youth leagues. But the ref hadn't blown the whistle.

The Wolves took the ball down to our basket, and one of them took a shot that bounced off the backboard. Bianca recovered it and dribbled down the court. I tried to get open, but as soon as I got near the basket I got swarmed again. Bianca passed it to Tiff, who made a two-point shot.

I slapped Tiff's hand as we hustled back. The Wolves passed the ball down the court this time, and took another shot. The ball careened off the backboard and there was a frenzy as both Nighthawks and Wolves went after it. The ball hit Dina's hands and flew out of bounds.

One of the Wolves threw it in to her teammate, who caught it and sank a shot close to the basket. Now the score was tied.

Tiff passed the ball in to me, and I tore down the court, determined to score this time. As soon as I got in the key, the wolf pack descended. I had no time to shoot, but I managed to get a bounce pass to Dina. She raced ahead with it so fast that she took some extra steps when she tried to shoot, and got called for traveling. The Wolves got the ball after that, and they brought it back down the court. One Wolf passed to her teammate, and got past us for a layup. Now we were down by two points.

The rest of the quarter was pretty frustrating. No matter what I did, I couldn't get free to shoot. It was like instead of a number I had a target on my uniform, and the Wolves were all out to get me!

As the first quarter came to an end, the score was Nighthawks 8, Wolves 12, and none of our eight points were mine. I had possession of the ball and was dribbling down the court when I heard Coach yell, "Elle, half court!"

I knew what she wanted me to do, and I didn't hesitate. I stopped right where I was and took the shot. It soared over the heads of the Wolves and into the basket. *Swish!* Then the buzzer rang. The quarter was over.

"Woo-hoo!" I cheered. It felt so good to finally make a basket, especially a three-pointer! I ran off the court, thirsty and sweaty.

"Coach, what is going on with their defense?" I asked. "Are they allowed to do that?"

Coach nodded. "The U.S. basketball rules allow double-teaming or crowding with players who are twelve or older," she said. "It's up to the coach's discretion. Most of the coaches in this region don't use it, but I think it's the Wolves' way of dealing with your height."

"Yeah, they're intimidated," Avery said.

I frowned. "Do you want me to sit out?"

Coach shook her head. "No way. Not until I have to. You're still getting rebounds, Elle. And you can use your long arms to steal the ball."

"What about scoring?" I asked. "Should I keep shooting from the foul line?"

"When I called for that shot right now, it was because we only had a few seconds left in the quarter, and I knew you could make it," she said. "But I don't want you shooting from there all the time. You should be drawing the foul."

I had totally forgotten about drawing the foul. I guess being away from the game for a few weeks had its drawbacks after all.

"You mean, take the shot, even if they're swarming

me, so that they foul me while I'm shooting," I said.

Coach nodded. "Right. You'll get free throws from that, and that will give us points."

I nodded. "Got it!"

The buzzer blared, and Coach put Hannah in for Bianca, Caroline for Avery, and Patrice in for Dina. League rules say that no player can play all four quarters, so I guessed that Coach was going to swap out players in the second and third quarters, and finish strong with the original five in the end.

When I ran out onto the court, though, my main thought was scoring. The first rebound I caught, I took off toward the Wolves basket. When I got into range, the Wolves defenders formed a circle around me again. Two of their players waved their arms in front of me, trying to block me from shooting.

Draw the foul, Coach had said, so I leaned into their arms and shot the ball. It bounced off the rim, missing the basket, but I heard the ref's whistle.

"Foul, Wolves!"

I jogged to the free-throw line and easily sank both of my free shots, for two points.

We pulled ahead of the Wolves in that quarter. Caroline caught a rebound and made a basket. I tossed a pass over the Wolves to Patrice, and with nobody guarding her, she made the shot. Hannah made a layup. I didn't have to draw the foul again, because twice I took the ball down the court, blowing past the defenders. Both times I shot and scored.

When halftime came, the score was Nighthawks 20, Wolves 18.

"I think the Nighthawks curse might finally be broken," Avery said to me, when I came off the court.

"Shh! Don't let Coach hear you," I whispered.

Coach called us into a circle for a talk.

"That was a strong quarter," she said. "Elle, you did a good job getting past their defense, but remember to keep drawing the foul if they're on you. I know I can count on you to make those free throws."

"Yes, Coach!" I replied.

"Now, you're all looking pretty good out there, but I do not want you to lose momentum," she went on. "Keep up the passing game. Don't lose focus on defense. And I don't want to see any more traveling violations today, okay?"

"YES, COACH!"

Coach benched me third quarter, like I thought she would. She put Bianca in as center and kept Hannah as shooting guard. Avery returned to play point guard. Caroline replaced Tiff, and Natalie replaced Patrice.

I took a seat on the bench next to Amanda, and I noticed that she wasn't smiling, like she usually is. In fact, she almost looked like she was going to cry.

"Are you okay?" I asked her.

"Coach didn't put me in," Amanda replied, without looking at me. "She left Hannah in. And I don't think she's going to use me in the last quarter."

"Maybe she forgot," I said. "She usually gives everyone a chance to play."

Amanda shrugged. "It's just weird, because before you came back Coach was putting me in as second center, and I was on the court all the time."

Her voice was tight, and I didn't know what to say. I mean, I understood why she was upset. If I had gone from being center to being benched, I would be upset too.

What I couldn't figure out was if she was upset with me, or with Coach. It didn't feel totally fair for her to be upset with me.

I pushed aside my worries about Amanda as I focused on the game in front of me. After just a few minutes, it seemed like the Wolves curse might be a real thing. The wolf pack had chosen Bianca as their new victim, and in her attempts to break away from them she ended up fouling twice! The Wolves started racking up points with foul shots. Coach had to call a timeout to remind Bianca to start drawing the foul, just like she had told me.

But we had lost our momentum. We couldn't seem to get a rebound, for some reason. Maybe it was just that the Wolves were being more aggressive to get the ball, but they always seemed to get possession, and kept scoring again and again. When the quarter ended, we had lost our lead: Nighthawks 29, Wolves 35.

"Elle, Bianca, Avery, Tiff, Dina, I want you all

in!" Coach yelled, and I avoided Amanda's eyes as I ran onto the court. It definitely looked like she wasn't going to get to play, unless Coach made a substitution. And with us down six points, that wasn't likely.

I looked at my four teammates. "Let's take this wolf pack down!" I said, and they all nodded, just as determined as I was to turn the game around.

Bianca threw me the ball and I raced down the court. The Wolves converged on me quickly, and I had to zigzag through them. Tiff was open so I passed it to her. She moved across the court but Wolves defenders stopped her, so she pivoted and passed it back to me. I was on the three-point line.

"Shoot, Elle!" Coach instructed.

I jumped. *Swish!* Three points!

"I have a new nickname for you, Elle," Dina called out as we jogged over to our basket. "Three-point Elle!"

That was a big improvement over the last nickname she had given me—the Runaway Train—after I'd spent a game running out of bounds. I grinned.

The Wolves missed their next shot, and Bianca took it down the court. The wolf pack went after her, and as I ran, I had an idea.

"Bianca, here!" I called out, waving my arms.

She couldn't get clear to pass to me, but that wasn't my plan. The pack turned their attention to me, freeing up Bianca. She took a shot and made it. Now we were only one point behind!

"Nice, Bianca!" I called out. I was drenched in sweat, but my energy was off the charts. I *knew* we could do this!

Avery scored next for us, and Dina got a point after one of the Wolves fouled her. Now the score was Nighthawks 37, Wolves 35, with four minutes left in the game.

The crowd might not have been big, but they started to get really excited once it began to look like the Nighthawks might finally beat the Wolves. I glanced up and saw a lot of people on their feet, even Mom and Dad!

I don't think I've ever felt so excited during a game! Did it make a difference? Maybe. Because

I scored again twice during the next four minutes, and so did Bianca.

"Biaaaaaaanca!" I cheered.

And the Wolves scoring streak had ended. Our defense was so tight!

"Block her!" I called to Dina, as the player in front of her moved left and right, trying to get past her. She gave up and let go of the ball, sending it wildly into the fray, and Avery scooped it up.

"Denied!" I cried. I was really enjoying seeing the downfall of the Wolves firsthand.

In the last seconds of the game, one of the Wolves tried for a three-point Hail Mary from the other side of the court. The ball didn't even reach the net. The final buzzer blared, and I looked at the scoreboard in disbelief. The final score was 44–35. Not only had we beaten the Wolves, we had beaten them by nine points!

The Nighthawks fans in the stands started screaming. *We* started screaming and jumping up and down. Then we composed ourselves long enough to slap hands with the Wolves. They really had played a great game.

Mom and Dad came out onto the court and hugged me.

"That was quite a return to the game," Dad said.

I nodded, still breathing heavily. "Yeah," I said. Then I glanced over and saw Amanda's sad face.

I should have felt great, but I didn't. I figured that Coach had put in the players she needed to so we could beat the Wolves. But I hated that Amanda hadn't been one of them.

It wasn't fair! Finally, I was having fun playing basketball, but my friend wasn't!

Are You Kidding Me?

H ey, why so sad? You guys beat the Wolves!"

I turned to see Kenya smiling at me, with Summer and Jenna next to her. I hugged them.

"It's so cool that you guys came!" I said.

"You're still our teammate, in spirit," Summer said.

"Yeah, even though you left us," Jenna said, her dark eyes twinkling. "But I guess it's good you did. I don't think your team could have beaten the Wolves without you."

"It was a team effort," I said.

As we talked, the members of the two boys' basketball teams streamed into the gym.

"Hey, me and some of my friends are going to stay to watch the boys' game," I said. "Want to hang out?"

Kenya looked at the other two girls, and they shrugged.

"Sure, why not?" Kenya said. "I'm curious to see if the boys can beat the Wolves too."

Jenna wiggled her fingers like she was some kind of magician. "Maybe the curse is broken," she said, in a spooky voice.

I laughed. "I'm going to get something from the snack table. See you in the bleachers!"

As I headed to the bench to grab my duffel bag, Blake ran up to me and held up his hand for a high-five.

"You guys did it! You beat the Wolves!" he said.

"Yeah, I guess we did," I said. "And you guys will too."

Blake's smile faded. "Oh man, I guess we have to now, right?"

"Don't think about it," I said. "Just play your best. Do it for Bianca." I smirked.

"Very funny," Blake said. "See you later!"

Then he ran off.

I jogged to the hallway to grab something from the snack table. It's run by parents and there's usually fruit, chips, protein bars, and stuff like that. I noticed that the hall was really crowded. I had to wait for, like, ten minutes just to get a protein bar.

Back in the gym, I spotted most of my team, still in uniform, sitting up near the top bleacher. My volleyball friends were hanging out near the bottom, so I grabbed them and brought them up with me to sit with the team.

I felt a little disappointed to see that Amanda wasn't there, and I made a mental note to reach out to her later. But now, the boys' game was about to start.

"Wow, there sure are a lot more people here than there were at our game," Bianca remarked from her perch on the bleacher behind me.

I turned to face her. "I was thinking the same

thing!" I said. "What's the deal with that?"

"People care more about boys' sports than girls' sports," Jenna chimed in. "It's a fact."

I thought about this. The words of the sportscaster popped into my head: *Pretty good, for a girls' team.* To me, that felt like proof that Jenna was right.

Kenya motioned to the boys' team warming up on the court. "I agree with Jenna. Did you know that the boys all got new uniforms this year?"

"The basketball team, you mean?" I asked.

"*Every* team," Kenya said. "And the girls haven't had new uniforms in like, eight years, my mom says. She was pretty upset about it. But when she asked the school about it, the school just said there was no budget for the girls' uniforms."

I frowned. "That doesn't seem right."

"Maybe we'll get some next year," Summer said hopefully.

Avery sighed. "I guess there's not much we could do about it, anyway."

Then the middle school cheerleaders ran out onto the court.

"Take it to the limit! Take it to the top! We're the mighty Nighthawks, and we can't be stopped!"

"'Top' and 'stopped' don't rhyme," Tiff muttered behind me.

Bianca looked at her. "Is that what's really bothering you? What about the fact that the boys have cheerleaders, and we don't?"

"I never really thought about that before," Tiff said. "Isn't it just the way things work?"

"It's just another example of what I'm talking about," Kenya said, and I nodded in agreement. Why hadn't I noticed all this before? Or maybe I had, and I just didn't want to admit to myself that things were so different for girls.

Then the buzzer blared, and the game started. As I watched, I tried to figure out if there was some way that the boys' game was more exciting than ours had been.

Were they scoring more? Not really. They did get called for traveling a few times, just like we did. Both teams committed fouls, just like we did. Yes, it was a pretty close game, but ours had been pretty close too.

The boys entered the fourth quarter with a four-point lead. The Spring Meadow fans started to get pumped up, stomping on the bleachers with their feet, when they realized that the Nighthawks might beat the Wolves. The cheerleaders were chanting nonstop.

"Go, fight, win! Go, fight, win!"

The Wolves scored at the start of the quarter. Then Blake made a layup. The Wolves scored again. The Nighthawks scored twice, lengthening their lead.

When the final buzzer rang, the Nighthawks had won with a score of 42–38. The crowd went crazy! Nighthawks fans ran out of the bleachers and swarmed the court. Me and my friends slowly made our way down to join them.

"The curse is over!" somebody shouted.

"The curse *was* over!" Bianca yelled into the crowd. "We beat the Wolves a couple of hours ago!"

But nobody heard her over the cheering. Kids were lifting up some of the boy players onto their shoulders.

"Nighthawks! Nighthawks! Nighthawks!" everybody was chanting.

"Um, where was this when you guys won?" Jenna asked.

"Nobody was here to do it," I said.

Avery tried to change the mood. "Hey, should we go out and celebrate our victory today?" she asked.

I shook my head. "Nah, Dad is swinging back here to bring me home," I said. I didn't really feel much like celebrating. I mean, I felt happy that both Nighthawk teams had won their games. But I was still feeling bummed about Amanda. And this whole thing with the boys' teams being treated better was messing with my mind.

Before I left, I found Blake.

"Awesome game!" I said, high-fiving him.

"Thanks," he said. "You guys broke the curse for us."

"There was never any curse," I told him. "Today, we were just better than them."

He grinned. "Yeah."

I said good-bye to Blake and headed outside to meet my dad.

"Thanks for picking me up," I said.

"No problem," he replied. "You can repay me by helping me make dinner."

I wiggled my eyebrows. "Does that mean you are going to give me your secret sauce recipe?"

"Never!" Dad joked. "But if you pay attention, you might learn a few things."

When we got home, I showered and walked Zobe before I settled in to the kitchen to help Dad. Beth was there, hanging with Mom, and Dad threw me an apron.

"Can you chop some carrots for me, Elle?" he asked.

"Sure," I replied, moving over to the cutting board. "Diced, or in coins?" I had learned a few things from Dad by helping him cook.

"Diced, please, Elle," he said, and I got to work.

Dad turned on the TV. "I want to check the local weather report. I heard that a cold spell is coming."

The local news station came on, and I heard someone say, "And now for our Sunday Sports Spotlight with Rob Robertson."

I looked up to see the same sports guy who had said, "Pretty good for a girls' team."

"Him again," I mumbled, and tried to tune him out as I chopped.

Then I heard Dad say, "Hey, look, it's the Night-hawks!"

I looked up to see Blake's team on the screen, in their game against the Wolves!

"Today we've got a story about a local rivalry," Rob was saying. "Fans sent in footage of the middle-school game between the Spring Meadow Nighthawks and the Wallton Wolves. The Nighthawks have not beaten the Wolves in more than twenty years, according to the legend, but today that curse was broken by the middle-school boys."

"What?" I shrieked at the screen. "Are you kidding?"

Everyone got quiet.

"So congratulations to the Nighthawks on their big win!" he finished.

I felt like throwing carrots at the screen, but I controlled myself.

"He must have received the fan video and didn't check the facts," Mom said, standing up. "I am going to e-mail the station right now."

"No," I said.

Mom looked puzzled. "No?"

"I'm going to do it," I told her. "It's *my* team he just disrespected."

"Good for you, Elle," Mom said. "Just try not to be angry when you write. Stay calm and you'll get your point across."

"I'll try," I promised, and after I finished chopping the carrots, some onions, and a bunch of parsley, I went up to my room and got out my laptop. I found the contact form on the News 12 website and started typing.

Rob Robertson just said that the Nighthawks boys' team broke the curse when they beat the Wallton Wolves. But he was wrong. The girls' team broke the curse in the game right before the boys. Can you please tell him he had a mistake?

I typed in my name and address. Maybe they would read it, and fix things. Maybe I would never hear back from them. Either way, I was glad I had stood up for the girls' team.

I felt even better after dinner, when I checked my laptop and found a reply from News 12.

Thank you for letting us know about the Nighthawks girls' team. We checked with the league and you are correct. We received several reports from people who were at the boys' game and so we assumed that they were factual. Rob will be making the correction during his report tomorrow. Congratulations on breaking the curse!

I jumped up. "Mom! Dad!" I ran downstairs with my laptop and showed them, excited.

"Nicely done, Elle," Mom said.

"Yes, good job," Dad said. "I'm proud of you."

"Thanks," I said. I felt like I had won a battle.

Then I thought about all the other things my friends had mentioned that day, like the uniforms, and the cheerleaders. Did I feel like taking on more battles, I wondered?

I already knew the answer. I was ready—and I knew where to start.

Dream Big

"**M**s. Ebear, can I talk to you?"

She looked up from her desk at me through her black eyeglasses—hipster glasses, Avery calls them. I just think they look cool.

"Sure, I've got a few minutes, Elle," she said. "What is it?"

I silently thanked Jim for agreeing to drive me and Blake in a few minutes early that morning. Both boys had complained about being tired, but tough. This was important.

"I don't know if this is a bullying issue, exactly,"

I began, "but me and some of the girls have been wondering why the girls' teams don't get treated the same as the boys' teams."

I told her about the uniforms. And the cheerleaders. And how everybody goes to the boys' games, but almost nobody comes to the girls' games. When I told her about how the news station had reported that the boys had broken the Wolves curse, she looked shocked.

"Wow, Elle, I can see why that would upset you," she said. "You make some really good points about the disparity between the two athletic programs, and the support they get."

I nodded. "Thanks. I guess I'm just wondering what to do about it."

Ms. Ebear frowned thoughtfully, tapping a pencil on her desk. "I think the first thing you might want to do is bring some of the girl athletes together. Don't try to take this on all by yourself. You have connections to both the volleyball and basketball teams, right? Start there."

I knew that some of my friends still thought

that the volleyball team had "stolen" me away from basketball, so I wasn't sure if they'd be thrilled to be working together. But it was worth a try. This was something we could all get behind.

"What kind of things do you think we could do?" I asked.

"You could always petition the school for new uniforms," she replied. "But as far as getting more people to support the girls' teams, you might want to start a booster club."

I knew what that was. My mom was part of the high school football booster club, although that was mostly parents. They raised money for the team, fed the boys when they traveled, and stuff like that.

"So if we started one, we'd be, like, supporting each other?" I asked.

Ms. Ebear nodded. "That's what I'm thinking. The basketball team could go to volleyball games, or softball games, and vice versa. You could decorate players' lockers like the cheerleaders do for the boys."

"Maybe we could ask the cheerleaders to cheer for us," I added.

She grinned. "That's the spirit, Elle! I think you're going to know what to do."

Some kids started coming into the room as homeroom neared.

"Listen, you might need an advisor for your group," she said. "I'd love to help but I'm really busy right now with the Buddy Club. Maybe ask one of your coaches?"

"Sure," I said. "Thanks for your help."

"No problem, Elle," she said. "I'm glad you asked."

And that is exactly why Ms. Ebear is my favorite teacher of all time!

When lunchtime came around, I brought up the idea to the girls on the team that I sit with: Avery, Natalie, Hannah, Caroline, and Patrice.

"A booster club," Avery repeated. "I like that idea."

Caroline nodded. "Me too. And I know we can definitely get Pete to be in it," she said.

I laughed. "I think he is our unofficial booster club right now anyway."

"So wait, we need to get together with the girls from the other teams?" Natalie asked.

"I thought we could start with the volleyball team, and then see if some of the other teams want to join us," I said. "Like cross-country, and track."

"How are we supposed to meet?" Hannah asked. "Our practice days are different than the volleyball practices."

"But we both have Saturday free," I said. "Ms. Ebear said we need an advisor, so we can't meet in the school until we figure that out. I was thinking we could just, like, maybe hang out on Saturday afternoon. Maybe at the diner?"

There are a few diners in and around Wilmington, but whenever you say "the diner" everybody knows what you mean: the River Queen Diner in North Creek. It's enormous, and they make the best cheese fries around.

Avery started making notes on her phone. She loves to organize things, and to my relief she swept in and started taking charge.

"Let's meet at the River Queen at two p.m. Saturday," she said. "Caroline, you talk to Bianca,

Tiff, and Dina. Elle, you talk to the volleyball team. Patrice, you can tell Amanda."

We just kind of sat there for a minute, thinking we could do it after lunch. But Avery had other ideas.

"What are you waiting for? Go! Everybody's here right now," she said.

I jumped up and saluted. "Yes, sir!" Then I bounded over to the volleyball team table.

Kenya, Summer, and Jenna were sitting with the rest of the team: Maggie, Taylor, and Lauren, the girl I had filled in for. They were all laughing loudly at something.

Jenna spotted me. "Hey, it's Elle! Please tell me you're coming back to the team."

"Yeah, we miss you, Ace," Maggie said.

"I miss you guys too," I said, sitting backward on a chair next to her. "But it feels good to be playing basketball again. I just really love it."

Summer looked at me. "You have to follow your truth, Elle."

"So what's up?' Kenya asked.

"I want to start a booster club for the girls' sports

teams," I began, and before I could say anything more, Kenya spoke up.

"Awesome! We're in!" she said. "This school really needs it."

The girls all high-fived me and then one another, cheering. Those volleyball girls had more positive energy than any other group I'd ever seen.

"Saturday, two o'clock, at the River Queen," I told them.

"Cheese fries!" Jenna cheered.

I headed back to my table to report to Avery and the others. On the way, I saw Patrice talking to Amanda. Until she joined the basketball team this year, Amanda wasn't really into sports. She plays clarinet in the school band, and at lunchtime, she sits with the band kids. She was smiling and listening to Patrice, and I was glad to see that she looked happier than she had after the game yesterday.

"The volleyball team is in," I reported when I sat back down at my lunch table.

Natalie gazed over at Kenya and the others, who were pounding their fists on the table and chanting, "Cheese fries! Cheese fries!"

"They sure are loud," Natalie remarked, and she rolled her eyes at Hannah. My worry that our two teams were going to be able to work together returned. Natalie and Hannah had been a little jealous of my friendship with the volleyball girls. Even Avery had questioned it.

But Avery said, "Maybe we *need* to make some noise right now. That's the whole point."

"Yeah," I agreed, and I started to feel really excited about our plans.

"I'm glad you're running the meeting, Elle," Avery said.

"Me?" I wasn't used to being the one in charge of things. How was I supposed to run the meeting? Couldn't we just hang out and talk it out?

Avery saw the look on my face. "I know a great app for making agendas."

I nodded. "Thanks. I can't do this alone!"

The rest of the week was focused on practice and schoolwork, because I knew I had a busy weekend ahead: a game on Sunday, a booster club meeting on Saturday afternoon, and on Saturday morning, the Buddy Club was getting ready for the takeover of the Valentine's Day Dance.

Going to the Buddy Club meeting meant that I was going to miss out on a training session with Dad and Zobe, but Dad had understood.

"I'll go over the lesson with you on Sunday night," he promised as he dropped me off at the school. Zobe whined in the back seat when I got out of the car, and I patted him on the head.

"I'll miss you, boy. Be good in school!"

He replied with a loud woof, and I laughed.

I made my way to Ms. Ebear's classroom, where I found all the kids from the Buddy Club, and a few extra ones. Katie, Gabrielle, and Dylan were busy cutting out paper hearts from construction paper, and Cole, Emily, Faith, and Satoko were writing messages on them with markers. They'd already finished a whole bunch of them, which I saw overflowing from two paper bags.

"Wow, you guys did so many already!" I exclaimed.

"We got a lot done on Wednesday," Ms. Ebear said, taking a sip of coffee. "I think we're ready to start putting them on lockers. Can I get a locker team going?"

I raised my hand, and so did Dylan, Katie, and Gabrielle.

"Great!" Ms. Ebear said. "Katie and Gabrielle, you do the sixth-grade lockers. Dylan and Elle, take the seventh grade. Then you can both tackle the eighth grade together. Come back here when you run out."

Ms. Ebear handed Dylan and Katie each a roll of masking tape, and she gave me and Gabrielle a bag of hearts. I riffled through them as Dylan and I made our way down the hallway.

The hearts were the same colors as those candy hearts—pink, yellow, light blue, and pale green. Curious to know what had been written on them, I started reading them aloud.

"'Make Today Great,'" I began. "'Today Is Your Day.' 'Believe in Yourself.'"

When we reached the seventh-grade lockers,

Dylan started breaking off pieces of the masking tape.

"I'll tape, you stick on the hearts?" he asked.

"Sure," I said, and we got to work.

"I guess this dance will be a lot less stressful than the cotillion," Dylan remarked.

"No kidding," I said.

"I mean, though, it wasn't *that* bad," Dylan said. "At least I had you as my partner."

"Yeah, sure," I said hesitantly. Where was Dylan going with this?

I handed him a paper heart, and my mind drifted off, thinking about the cotillion. I had been miserable, knowing I had to wear a dress. Avery had helped me out by bringing a sparkly hoodie for me to wear when the formal dance part was over, so I felt more like myself. And by then we could dance with whoever we wanted to, and I had danced with Amanda, jumping around and laughing. In the end, it had been really fun.

"Here's my locker," Dylan said, and I handed him one from the bag without looking.

"'You rock!'" he read. "Thanks, Elle."

I didn't have it in me to tell him that I had randomly picked it, but maybe I should have. Because then he did something that really surprised me.

"So, um, Elle," he said nervously. "Do you maybe want to, like, go to the dance together?"

Oh no! What was I supposed to say? Dylan is really nice, but I didn't like him like that.

"I don't know, Dylan," I said. "I mean, this is a Buddy Dance, right? I was just going to go with my friends."

"Yeah, right, of course," Dylan said quickly, and his cheeks turned pink. "A Buddy Dance. Duh."

"It was nice of you to ask, though," I said, which was true.

"Sure," Dylan said, but he was quiet as we made our way down the hall, until we came to my locker.

"Are you going to pick out something good for yours?" he said.

I dug my hand into the bag. "Nah, I'll just go for something random."

I pulled out a yellow heart that read DREAM BIG.

"Cool!" I said, and I slapped it onto the locker. *Dream big.* Like what I did when I imagined having my own line of women's pro basketball shoes. That was a big dream. *Dream big.* I could do that!

Dylan and I finished up the hall a few minutes later and went back to get more hearts. Katie and Gabrielle caught up to us and we breezed through the eighth-grade hallway while the others cleaned up the mess in Ms. Ebear's room. When we were all finished, we stepped out into the hallway to see our finished work.

"This looks amazing!" Satoko squealed.

"This will definitely get attention," Cole remarked. "Everybody's going to be talking about this on Monday morning."

"Principal Lubin is going to read our announcement on Monday," Ms. Ebear reported. "He told me that he's a hundred percent behind this change."

There was a pause, and it felt like we needed some kind of official moment of closure or celebration. I took a cue from my sports teams.

"Hands in!" I shouted, and I held out my right

arm. Everybody else figured it out, and we piled our hands on top of each other.

"Goooooo, Buddy Club!" I cheered.

"Goooooo, Buddy Club!" the others shouted, and we ended with a lot of whooping and clapping.

I couldn't stay to hang out much longer, though, because I had a booster club meeting to run. I just hoped that all my friends would be able to get along the way the Buddy Club did!

Experiment

So that will be six orders of cheese fries, twelve forks, six sodas, two iced teas, and four lemonades?" the waitress asked, repeating our order back to us. Her voice sounded flat, like she had taken a million orders like this before.

"That's right," Kenya told her.

"Coming up," she said, and then she quickly stepped away.

Almost all of us had been able to make it. Only Tiff, Caroline, Hannah, and Lauren couldn't be there. The twelve of us had moved three tables together in a corner of the diner, right in front of a huge painted wall mural of a steamship.

Now that our order had been taken, everyone looked at me.

"So, Elle, what's the plan?" Kenya said.

Thanks to Avery, I had a list of stuff to talk about on my phone. We had worked on it during the week, texting back and forth.

I looked down at my list. "First, we need an advisor. Ms. Ebear said we should ask one of our coaches."

Patrice spoke up. "I think my mom will do it. She was really happy when she heard we were forming a booster club."

"Yeah?" I asked. "Happy" was not a word I'd ever use to describe Coach Ramirez.

Patrice nodded. "Definitely," she said.

"We could ask Coach Patel, too," Kenya said. "He's really great." The volleyball girls nodded in agreement.

"Let's ask them both, and see who has the time to do it," Avery said.

"Plus, who says we can't have two advisors?" Hannah chimed in.

Everybody seemed satisfied with that, and I sighed with relief. I had been worried about the two teams getting along, but things were going great. I should have figured that girls who knew all about teamwork would be able to work together.

"Okay," I said, and I looked down at my list. "So, what kinds of things should we do?"

"We could start by going to each other's games and cheering each other on," Dina said.

"Definitely," Summer agreed.

Jenna spoke up. "I want cheerleaders, just like the boys have!"

"We should get *boy* cheerleaders," Natalie added, and Jenna grinned at her. Some of the girls started laughing. "They should have to wear short shorts just like the cheerleaders have to wear short skirts."

"Ew, no thank you!" I said. "Cheerleader uniforms are ridiculous. They're jumping around and doing amazing athletics. Shouldn't they be wearing sweats or leggings or something?"

"Well, Jenna's got a point," Avery said. "It's not fair that the boys get cheerleaders and we don't."

Amanda spoke up for the first time. "The other day, when Patrice came to talk to me, I was with some of my friends in the band," she said. "They said they would form a pep band for the girls' games."

"What's a pep band?" Jenna asked.

"It's a band that sits in the stands and plays, instead of marching on the field," Amanda explained. "You don't need a lot of musicians. So far we've got one drummer, a trumpet, a clarinet, and a flute. That should be enough to do some basic songs."

"I *love* that idea," I said, giving Amanda a grateful smile. "Much better than cheerleaders."

Then I winced. Had I insulted Jenna? I looked at her, and she was grinning.

"A band would be *awesome!*" she said. "The boys don't even have that."

Everybody started talking at once, excited by the idea of the pep band. Then our fries came, and everyone got *more* excited. When things calmed down, I went through my list, and we made some decisions.

We would try to meet every other Saturday after-noon. We would try to go to each other's games. We would decorate players' lockers before games. And we would reach out to the other girls' teams.

I was feeling pretty pumped up afterward, as we waited outside for our rides home.

"That went really well," I told Avery. "We made so many plans."

Then I had a panicked thought. "Oh no! I didn't write anything down. What if I don't remember everything? There was the pep band, and the lock-ers, and . . ."

"Chill," Avery told me. "I took notes on my phone."

I hugged her. "What would I do without you?"

Then I heard someone call out, "Bye, Amanda!" and I turned to see Amanda climbing into her mom's car. She hadn't even said good-bye to me before she left, which was unusual.

That deflated my happiness bubble a tiny bit, but not much. I still had a great feeling after our meet-ing. A positive feeling that by working together, we could make a change. Was it girl power? Whatever it was, I couldn't wait for tomorrow's game!

Sunday began like every other game day. I woke up at 6:30 and walked and fed Zobe. Then I spent thirty minutes shooting baskets in my driveway. After that, I showered, ate half a bagel with peanut butter, and napped for a half hour. When I woke up, I put on my jersey, basketball shoes first. Then I put on my shorts, right foot first, so I would be sure to start off the game on the right foot.

Mom and Dad drove me to the game in Hillside, where we were playing against the Gophers.

"Will your booster club be in full force at the game?" Mom wanted to know.

"I'm not sure," I admitted. "We only had one day to plan. I'm not sure if the other girls are ready to come support us yet. But there's still time in the season."

When we got there, only about half of the Nighthawks were there, and the stands were about as empty as they always were. When the whole team was there, we warmed up with a shooting drill, and

I wasn't thinking about the booster club at all until the sound of a trumpet made me jump.

I turned to see four musicians from the band sitting in the stands, wearing Nighthawks T-shirts. They were playing "Another One Bites the Dust." Amanda smiled and waved at them.

"Wow, they're really great!" I said.

She nodded. "Yeah, I told them that they need to be quiet when we were playing, because they sound so loud in here. But they can play for us during breaks and stuff. And to get the game going."

I bit my lip. "I hope Coach doesn't mind."

But when I looked over at her, Coach was tapping her foot to the music.

The second surprise came when the girls from the volleyball team came in with a few other girls from our school. They were holding up a paper banner: GO, NIGHTHAWKS! They brought it up to the top of the stands, and it looked *amazing*!

Coach talked to us before we went out onto the court.

"I normally don't talk about stats, but today is

a big game," she said. "If we win today, we will be guaranteed a spot in the playoffs."

Some of the girls cheered. Avery and I looked at each other, our mouths open.

"If we make it, this will be the first time the seventh-grade team has gone to the playoffs," she said.

"No way. Really?" Natalie asked.

"Really," Coach replied. "So no excuses today. Go out there and play your best!"

"YES, COACH!"

I wondered why Coach had given us this news right before the game. It was a lot of pressure—but it was also a huge motivation. Because we did play our best—all of us. The band and the banner and the girls cheering us on really helped too.

Caroline scored a free throw. Avery made two layups. Patrice made an awesome shot after she recovered a rebound. Coach put in Amanda in the third quarter, and she blocked two shots from the Gopher girl she was guarding. The third time, she stole the ball and passed it to Bianca, who made a basket.

I played one of my best games yet. I scored fifteen points! In the end, we beat the Gophers 43–30.

After the game, the pep band launched into a happy victory song. The volleyball girls came down with the banner and swarmed us. It felt like a big win—bigger than beating the Wolves. We were the first seventh-grade team to make it to the playoffs!

"You guys are coming out to celebrate with us, right?" I asked Kenya.

"Definitely!" Kenya replied, and a little while later we were all in the crowded pizza parlor, hyped up and making a lot of noise. I looked around at all the girls, and thought about the yellow heart on my locker: *Dream Big*. The booster club idea had started out as a kind of a dream. And now it was really working!

I turned to talk to Kenya at the table behind me. "Thanks for the banner. That was really cool."

Kenya grinned. "You guys can borrow it for Friday if you want."

Avery overheard us. "We should surprise you with something, just like you surprised us."

"I hope you have an idea," I whispered to Avery.

"Don't sweat it," she told me. "We'll figure it out."

The pep band had come out with us too—two boys and two girls—and Amanda was sitting with them at a table. I walked over. I knew their names, because this is a small school, but I didn't know them that well.

"You guys sounded awesome," I said. "Thanks so much."

"No problem," said Kyle, the drummer.

"We don't get to play much now that football season is over," added Stephen, who played clarinet.

"Yeah, and it's easier than marching around the field," added Kristin, the flute player.

Rachel, the trumpet player, nudged Amanda. "I just wish Amanda was still playing with us."

"Hey, I'm still in the concert band!" Amanda said. "And I'm in the orchestra for the spring musical, too."

"Wow, that's like, a lot of music-playing," I said, and then I cringed. Had I forgotten how to make sentences all of a sudden? .

"Thanks," Amanda said, and then she looked away from me and started talking to Rachel about the musical.

"Okay then, well, thanks," I said. "Will you guys be at the volleyball game on Friday?"

Kyle nodded. "Yup," he said. Then he tapped on the table with his drumsticks.

I felt a little sad as I walked back to the table. My friendship with Amanda just wasn't the same, and I wasn't sure why.

Our friendship needs a booster club, I thought, which was kind of a silly thought, but it gave me an idea for a way to make things better. Because even though things were going really great, I knew they could be much better if I could fix things with Amanda.

Jealous? Seriously?

G ood morning, Spring Meadow!" Principal
Lubin announced over the speakers. "I am
sure you were *heartily* surprised to see the
wonderful hearts on your lockers this morning. The
members of the Buddy Club put their *heart* and soul
into them and wanted me to announce that this
year's middle school Valentine's Day Dance now
has a *heart*-warming theme: friendship! That's right.
Cupid is taking a vacation, and this year's dance will
be a Buddy Dance. From the bottom of my *heart*, I
think this is a great idea!"

I looked at Ms. Ebear. Principal Lubin's corniness could be painful sometimes. He was the king of dad jokes.

"That is *not* what Cole wrote," she said. "But I think he got the point across."

She was right. Even Principal Lubin's cringeworthy delivery could not spoil the excitement over the revised Valentine's Day Dance. It was all anybody could talk about on Monday. People were asking one another what message they got. Most were really relieved that the dance was no longer a romantic one—except for a few eighth-graders. Word got around that Lanie Frye said that a Buddy Dance was too immature, and she tried to get a petition going to keep it a Valentine's Day Dance. But I heard that she only got four signatures. Most people really loved our idea.

At practice that day, we got more good news.

"The Wolves lost their game this weekend," Coach Ramirez announced before practice started. "If we win our next game—which is our last regular season game—we'll get the home-court advantage on the playoff schedule. That's a big deal. So this is not the time to slack. Give me twenty!"

It was just like Coach to double our laps while we were on top of our game, but none of us minded.

"We're going out on top!" Natalie sang happily as she and Hannah jogged past me.

Bianca caught up to me. "You came back just in time, Elle," she said, and I smiled at her.

"Just don't mess it up!" she concluded, before jogging ahead. It didn't bother me. That was just Bianca being Bianca.

I got a ride home from Avery's mom after practice, and I ran into the house, excited. Zobe jumped up and licked my face. I patted him and went to Beth and formed into her hand: *Happy*. I knew she liked to know when I got good news.

"You seem very cheerful, Elle," Mom said.

"The team is doing great," I told her. "We've got one more game before the playoffs, and if we win, we'll get the home-court advantage. And I think we can do it. We've gotten so good at working together."

She looked at me. "So I guess you're glad you rejoined the team?"

"I am," I said. "And not just because we're winning. I'm really having fun."

"I'm glad you found your way back," Mom said. "Now please feed Zobe!"

My poor dog's pre-dinner whine was becoming deafening, so I quickly obeyed.

"Things are a little crazy right now, Zobe, but I'll make it up to you," I promised. And I did, with an hour-long play session in the living room after dinner, because it was too cold to go outside.

The next day after school, I went to Avery's house to make a sign for the volleyball team. Patrice, Natalie, Hannah, Dina, and Tiff came too. Avery had stacked her kitchen table with art supplies: poster paper, construction paper, markers, and stickers.

"We need to do something really cool," I said. "The banner that the volleyball team made for us was awesome."

"Well, we have one thing that they don't have,"

Avery said, and I noticed that both her hands were behind her back.

"What's that?" Natalie asked.

Avery grinned and thrust out her arms. "Glitter!"

She held two giant jars of glitter—one green, and one yellow.

Tiff made a face. "Glitter is sooooooo messy! Somebody gave me a birthday card with glitter in it once, and I kept finding it in my hijab, no matter how much I washed it!"

"It's messy but it's beautiful," Natalie said.

"Well, maybe we could just do the *N* in Night and the *H* in Hawks, in glitter," Avery suggested.

"Let's do the letters first and see how they look," Hannah suggested.

Avery nodded. "Great," she said. "And I thought we could do individual locker signs for each of the players. Elle, you know them better than anybody here. Can you take charge of that?"

"Sure," I replied.

"When are we going to put these up?" Hannah asked.

"I was thinking that everybody could get to school early on Friday," Avery replied. "Or at least a few of us."

"I can probably do it," I offered. "It won't take long."

"Great. Then I'll definitely help," Avery said.

Tiff and Patrice helped me with the individual posters. We made one each for Kenya, Summer, Jenna, Maggie, Taylor, and Lauren.

"What should we do? Draw volleyballs?" Patrice asked.

Tiff tapped a marker on the table. "Maybe we should add some volleyball sayings." She looked at me. "Are there volleyball sayings?"

I had been on the team long enough to know the answer to that.

"We could do 'Serve it up!'" I suggested.

"We should put that one on Kenya's because she's a great server. Then there's 'Block this!' Or 'Can you dig it?' Dig it, because a dig is when you dive to keep a spiked ball from hitting the floor."

"Perfect," Tiff said. "We need some stickers,

too. Avery, what kind of stickers do you have?"

"Come see," Avery said, and Tiff and I rummaged through the sticker pile. She had three sheets of glittery volleyballs, as well as hearts, stars, and stickers with sayings on them like, "Go Team!"

"Where did you get all this stuff?" I asked.

"Mom took me to the craft store," she said. "We go there, like, once a week anyway. I love this kind of stuff."

"I know," I said. "You should totally be booster club president."

Avery's eyebrows shot up. "Really? I mean, I know this was kind of your idea, and you led the meeting and everything . . ."

"Do you remember who you're talking to?" I asked. "I am the one who has too much to do and no organizational skills. I think you would be an awesome president."

"Avery for president!" Natalie yelled.

"Well, I think we need to talk to the others . . . ," Avery said.

"I'll bring it up at our next meeting," I said. "But

once the volleyball team sees everything we've put together, I'm sure you'll get their vote."

Avery beamed, and that made me happy. I could tell that she was doing something she really loved.

We finished the banner and the posters in about an hour, and I stayed behind to help Avery clean up. As we worked, I put aside some paper, stickers, and a glitter pen.

"Do you mind if I take this home?" I asked.

"Sure. What for?" Avery asked. "Oh wait. Are you making a Valentine for someone?"

I felt myself blush. It freaks me out how Avery can be almost psychic sometimes. "Sort of. Not really. Kind of," I replied.

Avery laughed. "Whatever. Have fun with it!"

The rest of the week flew by. I worked on my special project. We practiced for Sunday's game. And on Friday, the day of the volleyball game, Avery and I got to school early.

"Kenya's locker is over here," I said as we got ready to put the first poster up.

We worked fast, and we finished before other kids started arriving at school. I darted off to put something in a different locker. Then Avery and I hung out in the hallway and waited.

Summer arrived first. We watched her walk to her locker, and then she let out a squeal.

"I love it!"

Avery and I high-fived. A few girls headed to Summer's locker to check out her poster. Then we heard Jenna yell.

"I got one too!"

Soon the whole volleyball team was dashing around the hallway, checking out the posters. Then Kenya spotted me and Avery and walked up to us.

"Nice job," she said. "Thanks!"

"Wait till you see our banner," Avery teased.

We all headed to homeroom together, and we passed Jordan and Ethan, two boys on the basketball team with Blake.

"Yo, who did the posters for you?" Jordan asked Kenya, and we all stopped.

"The girls' basketball team," she told him. "We

formed a booster club, so we can support each other's teams."

"So do the boys get posters?" Ethan asked.

"No, that's kind of the whole point," Avery chimed in. "You guys already get new uniforms, and cheerleaders, and better news coverage."

"Yeah, but we don't get posters," Jordan said.

Kenya gave him a look. "Are you serious? You're jealous of a *poster*?"

"I didn't say we were jealous," Jordan argued. "Just that . . . whatever, forget it."

"We will," Kenya promised them, and she walked away. Avery and I followed her.

"Can you believe those boys?" she asked. "Jealous of a poster, with all the stuff they get."

"Well, they *are* awesome posters," I joked, and Kenya just shook her head.

I guess it was flattering that the boys wanted posters too. Everybody noticed them, and it really helped get people excited about the game. After basketball practice that afternoon, we all hurried home to eat and get changed before the girls' volleyball game. Dad dropped me off back at the school at seven o'clock.

Avery and Patrice were already there, holding up the glittery Nighthawks banner. The pep band was playing. A bunch of girls from the track team climbed up onto the bleachers to sit with them.

"Kenya told us about the booster club," said one of the girls. "We want to help."

"Awesome," Avery said. "Right now, all you have to do is cheer."

I slid onto the bleachers next to Avery. From our perch, we could see people streaming into the gym. It was definitely a bigger crowd than we'd ever had at a girls' volleyball game before.

"It's working!" I told Avery, and she replied with a giant grin.

Then I spotted Amanda entering the gym. I was a little nervous about seeing her, because she hadn't said much to me during practice. And I had been waiting all day to see what she would think of my peace offering. Since she hadn't said a word, I'd been thinking that she didn't like it.

I expected her to sit with the band, but instead she climbed up and sat next to me.

"Hi," she said shyly.

"Hi," I replied.

She reached into the pocket of her hoodie and pulled out a folded piece of construction paper. The same paper I had put in her locker that morning. She unfolded it.

I'd used the art supplies I'd borrowed from Avery to make a card for Amanda. A card that I just happened to give her on Valentine's Day. With stickers of hearts and stars making funny faces, and a glittery border. I had written the letters of her name down the paper.

Always smiling
Makes me laugh
Asks me how I'm doing
Never gives up
Dogs love her and she loves dogs
Amanda!

"Your name has a lot of *A*s," I told her. "It was hard to think of a third one for the last line."

"I like it," she said. "That was sweet, Elle."

I shrugged. "I know it's goofy. I just . . . I kind of felt like we're not friends anymore, and that made me sad."

Amanda nodded. "I know. It's complicated, I guess. It's just . . ."

Before she could finish, the volleyball teams ran out onto the court. Avery and Patrice stood up.

"Nighthawks! Nighthawks!"

All the Nighthawks fans in the stands joined the chant.

"Nighthawks! Nighthawks!"

Then the game began, and the action just didn't stop. Kenya kept making killer serves that landed just inbounds. Summer spiked the ball so fast the players on the opposing team looked shocked. Jenna kept setting up beautiful passes for her teammates to get over the net.

"This is more action-packed than I thought it

would be," Avery whispered to me during the game.

"Yeah, it's much more intense than gym volley-ball. There's a lot more skill to it than I realized," I said, and she threw me a look of alarm. "But I have more fun playing basketball."

"Good to know," she replied.

We all cheered the Nighthawks girls' team to a win. When the game finished, I wanted to take Amanda aside and finish our conversation. But she darted away before I could.

"Hey!" I called after her. "See you at the dance tomorrow?"

"Nope!" she called back. "I hate dances!"

Kenya ran up to me, grabbed my arm, and swung me around.

"We are doing it, Elle!" she cheered. "The girls are killing it!"

"Yes we are!" I cried. "Great game!"

Our plan to boost the girls' teams was a success. That was good. But for the rest of the night, all I could think about was: *What did Amanda want to tell me?*

The Buddy Dance

So everybody agrees that Avery can be the booster club president?" I asked.

The girls gathered at the River Queen Diner all replied "yes" in one way or another.

"Great. Thanks!" Avery said. "And Coach Ramirez and Coach Patel both said they would be our advisors. So we can meet in the school if we need to."

"But then we wouldn't get cheese fries!" Jenna shouted.

"The diner is going to have to build an addition

if we keep meeting here," Tiff said. Four of the girls from the track team had joined us, and now we took up six tables.

My phone alarm went off, and I stood up. "Gotta run," I said. "I have to go help the Buddy Club set up for the dance."

"See you later, Elle!" Avery called out.

I waved good-bye to everybody and headed outside, where Dad was waiting to drive me to the school. When I got there, Ms. Ebear and Principal Lubin were supervising the members of the Buddy Club setting up for the party.

"Oh good, Elle's here!" Cole said.

"Uh, hi!" I said. Why was Cole so excited to see me?

"We need somebody tall to put up the streamers," he said. "Even with the ladder, I'm too short."

What could I say? I wasn't insulted. Sometimes it comes in handy to be tall. I took a roll of yellow streamers from him.

"How do you want me to do this?" I asked.

Cole and Emily gave me instructions, and I

moved around the gym with the ladder, draping the streamers over and under the metal rafters. It took kind of a long time, but the end result was pretty spectacular. It looked like a bunch of rainbows were hanging over the gym.

"This looks great, everyone!" Ms. Ebear said. "It's time for dinner break. I'll see you back here at seven for the dance."

"Ms. Ebear, shouldn't we teach Elle the—you know, the surprise?" Satoko asked.

"Oh, that's right!" Ms. Ebear said. "Elle, we worked out a little surprise for tonight at Wednesday's meeting. There's not much time, but we could teach it to you if you like."

"What kind of surprise?" I asked, and she explained it to me.

I smiled. "Wow, that's cool. But totally do it without me. I don't think I'd have time to learn it."

"You sure?" Dylan asked.

I nodded. "Sure!"

Dad brought me home for a quick dinner and I changed into my outfit for the dance: a clean pair of jeans and a Nighthawks T-shirt. Mom gave me a look when I walked down the stairs, but she didn't argue. Even so, I started to defend myself.

"It's not even a Valentine's Day Dance anymore, it's a Buddy Dance," I reminded her. "The theme is friendship. It's casual."

"I'm sure many of the other kids will still be getting dressed up, though, Elle," Mom said. "Are you sure you won't feel uncomfortable?"

"Are you kidding? I am *beyond* comfortable!" I told her. I slipped on my coat and hugged her. "See you later!"

When I walked back into the gym, it looked even nicer than it had before, with the lights dimmed and a spinning spotlight casting a colorful glow around the room. Some volunteer parents were serving water, hot cocoa, and cookies to the kids who had arrived. Pop music blared from a speaker.

Avery came running up to me. She looked adorable, in a white dress with little pink hearts, and pink flats.

"You are too cute," I told her. "But you know

this isn't a Valentine's Day Dance anymore, right?"

She shrugged. "It's still kind of a Valentine's Day Dance," she said. "At least *I'm* dressed for a dance."

I punched her arm. "I can dance perfectly fine in this. Although I don't necessarily plan to dance."

Avery gazed around. "It doesn't look like anyone else is, either," she said.

Even though this was supposed to be a Buddy Dance, where everybody could hang out with their friends, the girls were gathered at one side of the gym, and the boys were on the other. And nobody was dancing.

I smiled. "I have a feeling that might change soon."

Like magic, as soon as I said it, loud rock music came blaring from the speakers. Dylan, Cole, Katie, Gabrielle, Satoko, Emily, and Faith ran out into the center of the gym. They got in a line and started dancing.

It looked like one of those flash mobs you see online, where people start doing choreographed dance moves and surprise everyone around them.

My Buddy Club friends were swaying from side to side, hopping from left to right, and clapping their hands in perfect time. It looked like fun, but I was kind of glad I hadn't been able to practice it with them. I'm pretty sure I would have tripped over my own feet!

After a few moves, everybody watching started clapping and cheering. They moved away from the walls of the gym and toward the dance floor to watch. Then Ms. Ebear and Principal Lubin ran out and joined the line and started dancing with them! Everyone went really crazy after that.

When the song finished, the Buddy Club members took a bow, and a new song started.

"Come on and dance everybody!" Cole called out. "Dance with a friend!"

Avery grabbed my arm. "Come on, friend!" she said, and she pulled me out onto the dance floor.

We ran toward Natalie and Hannah. Natalie wore a pink skirt that matched the pink streak in her hair, and Hannah had on a cute blue dress. That's when I realized that Mom was right—most kids did get dressed up. Some of the boys were even wearing ties!

We all started dancing. Dina danced over to us, twirling around like a tornado. Patrice was bopping up and down. The pool of girls and the pool of boys combined into one big sea of kids, and almost everybody was dancing.

I scanned the crowd, hoping that Amanda had changed her mind, but I didn't see her. I totally understood why she didn't like going to dances, but I knew she would have liked this one. It definitely didn't feel like a regular dance.

However, we were a roomful of middle schoolers, so there had to be some awkward moments, right? At one point, some of the eighth-grade boys and girls started dancing together. When that happened, some of the seventh-grade boys and girls did the same—like Blake and Bianca.

That's when I saw Dylan zigzagging his way toward me. He was one of the dressed-up kids, in a pale yellow shirt and green tie to match the hearts on the wall. He had a look on his face that told me exactly what he planned to do. My stomach sank.

"Wanna dance?" he asked me.

Over the next three seconds, I held a rapid-fire debate with myself. This was a Buddy Dance. Dylan was my buddy. So why not dance with him? But if I danced with him, he might think I liked him. Like, *liked* him. Which I did not. But it was a Buddy Dance. . . .

"Okay," I said. "But you know I'm a terrible dancer."

He grinned. "So am I," he said. "But I've been, uh, practicing."

To my complete surprise, Dylan started to do that dance where you swing your arms back and forth across your body while swinging your hips from side to side.

"You're flossing!" I said.

Dylan blushed. "Am I doing it wrong?"

"No, it's perfect," I said. "I have never been able to figure it out."

I tried it, and even though I couldn't see myself, I knew I was doing it wrong.

"See? I can't do it!" I said, laughing.

Dylan stopped moving.

"Keep going!" I urged him.

Dylan launched into his dance. Some other kids noticed and a circle formed around him. I stepped back, out of the way.

Awkward couples dance averted, thanks to Dylan's flossing skills!

Blake approached me. "Your boyfriend's a good dancer."

"He's NOT my boyfriend," I said, giving him a shove.

Blake held up two hands. "Okay! Okay! Calm down." He changed the subject. "I heard there's a pep band coming to your games."

I nodded. "Yeah, they're Amanda's friends. They're helping out the booster club."

"I wish we had a pep band," he said.

I rolled my eyes. "Not you, too! You already get cheerleaders and new uniforms and more people come to your games. You know that, right?"

Blake slowly nodded. "Yeah, I guess you're right. I never really thought of that before."

"It's not just high school, you know," I said. "I've been looking stuff up. Let's say we both go on to play pro basketball after college."

"Okay," Blake said.

"Your salary would be something like half a million dollars," I said.

Blake raised his eyebrows. "Seriously?"

"Seriously," I said. "But if I was starting in the WNBA, I would make fifty thousand. That's ten times less than what you would make!"

"You're kidding," Blake said.

"No, it's real," I told him. "Even refs in the NFL make more than WNBA players. Refs!"

"Okay, that is straight up weird, because first of all, you are a better basketball player than me," Blake said.

I nodded. I wasn't being conceited; that was just a fact.

"People say that NBA players get paid more because their games earn more money. They get more fans and more advertisers," I went on. "And yeah, that's true. But is it because the guys' games are more exciting? Or because women's sports don't get enough attention—not in the pros, and not in schools."

Blake shook his head. "You definitely deserve a pep band. You deserve more than a pep band."

"Yeah!" I said.

Avery walked up to us. "What do you deserve?"

"Cookies!" I said, grabbing her by the arm. "Let's go get some cookies!"

We raced across the gym, and I thought about how tomorrow, I'd be racing across a gym with a basketball. It wasn't all about a pep band, or cheerleaders, or whether I would someday be in the WNBA.

It was about winning for the Nighthawks.

The Ball Stealer

Those are the Mavericks? They look small," Avery said.

I dropped my duffel bag on the visitor's bench and followed her gaze to the opposite side of the Middletown Middle School gym. The Maverick girls' team was warming up with stretches.

"You think?" I asked.

"Definitely," she said. "Look at them compared to their coach. None of them are as tall as she is, and she's not even as tall as you!"

"You're right, but it's weird," I said. "There are

some schools where the girls are all really tall. And now here they're all shorter. What's up with that?"

Avery shrugged. "I don't know, but a team of shorties is a slam dunk for us," she said, and she high-fived me.

"Come on, Avery," I said. "I know better than anybody that you should never judge anybody based on their height, right?"

She sighed. "Sure, get all mature on me!"

"Nighthawks on the court!" Coach Ramirez barked.

We all scrambled onto the court and launched into a shooting drill. While we warmed up, the volleyball team arrived with a bunch of girls from the track team, and a banner. The pep band kids came and started to play.

Avery shot a basket and ran down the sidelines. "Nice banner!" she called up to Kenya. "But where's the glitter?"

"We've got something better than glitter!" Kenya shouted back.

She motioned to the band, and they stopped

playing. Then she and the other girls stood up and started clapping. Then they began to chant.

>*"Come on, Nighthawks!*
>*Let us hear that sound we love.*
>*I'm saying Swishhhhhhhh!*
>*Swishhhhhhhh!*
>*Let us see two points.*
>*Two points on the board.*
>*I'm saying Swishhhhhhh!*
>*Swishhhhhhh!"*

I couldn't believe it. They swung from side to side whenever they said "Swishhhhhhh!" It was awesome!

We all started clapping, and Kenya and the girls high-fived each other.

"We're going to have to beat that at the next volleyball game!" I told Avery.

While we did our shooting drill, the stands kept filling up. Jim came with Mom and Dad. Caroline's family was there, with Pete, my personal cheerleader. And right before the game started, Blake showed up, with five boys from the basketball team!

"No way!" I said. Blake gave me a thumbs-up. My heart melted. I was so lucky to have a great friend like him! I had no idea how he convinced the boys to come with him, but I was glad that he had.

Coach Ramirez called us into a huddle.

"I want everyone to give one hundred percent today," she said. "When we win this game, we will be in a great position to start the playoffs. I've seen the Mavericks play, and they're fast! I want to see a tight passing game today. Got it?"

"YES, COACH!" we replied. Then we put our hands in for a cheer. "Gooooooo, Nighthawks!"

The buzzer blared and we ran out onto the court: me, Bianca, Tiff, Avery, and Dina. I faced off against the Mavericks center. The top of her curly red hair barely reached the nape of my neck. I couldn't help thinking that maybe Avery was right. Was this going to be an easy win?

The ref threw up the ball, and I reached it easily before the center, number 17, did. I batted it sideways to Bianca and ran forward. Bianca passed it right back to me.

Only I didn't catch it. Number 17 darted in front of me and grabbed the ball before I could! She dribbled down the court, hugging the right sideline. I tried to catch up to her but Coach was right—she was fast! Then she stopped and made a short pass to one of her teammates, who dribbled up to the basket and made a layup. The Mavericks had scored first!

Avery took the ball out and passed it to me. I charged across the court, making it to the Mavericks basket in four bounces. I stopped and dribbled once to prep for my shot. The ball bounced off the floor but didn't reach my fingers. 17 had stolen it away from me!

"Elle, keep the ball close to you!" Coach yelled, and I nodded, feeling a little bit in shock. Was this girl some kind of magician?

The Mavericks made their way down the court with four short, tight passes. This time, Tiff blocked their shot attempt and hurled a long pass down the court to Avery. It hit the top of Avery's fingers and bounced out of bounds.

The Mavericks had control and missed another shot attempt. Dina caught a rebound and dribbled it, then passed it to Bianca. I used my long legs to my advantage and blazed past 17. Seeing me open, Bianca passed me the ball.

I dribbled toward the basket, and 17 was right on me. I tried to zigzag around her but I tripped and ended up on my knees. Great! But I still had the ball. Twisting around, I passed it to Avery. She took a shot and made the basket. The game was tied, 2–2.

Coach Ramirez called a timeout.

"These girls are all over the ball," she told us. "Pass high, not low. Elle, when you're dribbling, aim for better control. Don't give her a chance to steal it from you. And when they're in shooting range, block them!"

I nodded. "Yes, Coach!" Then I took a quick swig of water before we went back in.

Avery passed the ball to Bianca. She lobbed it over the head of her defender to Dina, who fumbled it.

There was a mad scramble as everyone on both teams tried to get the ball. One of the Mavericks got it and rocketed down the court. She shot, missed, and 17 got it. I moved right in front of her and mirrored her moves as she tried to reach the basket. Finally, she twisted around and passed to a girl behind her.

The defensive possession felt good, but I wanted to score! I had my chance when I caught a pass from Avery, but I shot too far to the left. Tiffany scored before the quarter ended, but so did the Mavericks. We went into the second quarter with a 4–4 score.

I say "we," but Coach didn't put me in. She benched me, probably unsure if I could handle 17. But the Mavericks moved 17 to Bianca, and 17 stole the ball from her twice. So it wasn't just me. At the end of the second quarter, the score was Nighthawks 14, Mavericks 16.

Bianca came back to the bench, shaking her head. "That girl is unbelievable," she said.

I nodded. "Yeah, I don't know what to do about her. She's relentless!"

"Well, I hope Coach puts you back in, so she'll

be your problem again," Bianca said with a grin. Her wish came true. Third quarter it was me, Avery, Dina, Caroline, and Amanda. The Mavericks still had 17 in there.

I tried a new strategy. Since shooting is my strength, I took a shot whenever I got close to the key, before 17 had a chance to get in front of me. I made four out of the seven baskets I attempted. I'm not sure if that was Coach's plan, but she didn't complain. The Mavericks might be fast, but at least I could shoot over all their hands!

The third quarter ended in a tie, 28–28. Coach put me back in, and I was psyched. I wanted to finish out this game! I ran onto the floor with Bianca, Amanda, Patrice, and Tiff.

Number 17 was benched, and they put number 23 on me, a girl who wasn't much taller than her teammate. She stole the ball from me once, right after I caught a pass from Tiff. That was the only time I let that happen. I stuck to my strategy of shooting whenever I was free, and racked up five points pretty quickly. Nighthawks 33, Mavericks 28.

Then the Mavericks had the ball in the key. Number 23 passed to 4. She passed to 6. She passed it back to 4. She passed it to 12.

I launched myself in front of 12 as she shot the ball, and stumbled. I felt my elbow jab right into her side right before I saw the ball sink through the net. The ref blew his whistle. I had fouled the shooter.

Number 12 made her free throw to give the Mavericks an extra point. Now the game was 33–31. Too close. In the stands, our friends were stomping and yelling, "Go, Nighthawks!"

The next time we had the ball, I took it to the foul line and stopped. I had a clear shot, but Amanda was right under the basket, open. I passed it to her. She leaped up and sank the ball.

"Swiiiiiiiiiiiiiiish!" yelled Kenya and the other girls. Amanda beamed at me and I slapped her hand.

Now we had a four-point lead: 35–31. The clock ticked down. Bianca tried to score and missed. The Mavericks kept up their passing game and scored. We took it back across the court and Patrice lost control of the ball. The Maverick player next to her grabbed the ball and passed it. Patrice leaped and stole it! Then she dribbled past the startled Mavericks and made a layup.

We were back up by four points. But the Mavericks came back strong, scoring twice, so quickly we didn't know what happened. The game was tied, 37–37.

We got the ball back. Patrice passed it to me and I dribbled down the court. I stopped just before the three-point line and decided to shoot. I felt a tug on my jersey and watched the ball miss the basket.

Tweet! One of the Mavericks had fouled me. Because I was in the three-point zone, I got to make three free throws, and I wanted every one of them to count.

The crowd got quiet—eerily quiet. I tried not to think about them and focused on the basket. I took a deep breath and shot.

Swish!

"Swiiiiiiiiish!" my friends yelled in the stands.

I bounced the ball a few times and took my second free throw.

Swish!

"Swiiiiiiiish!"

Now the crowd started to make noise. People were clapping, stomping, and cheering. I know they didn't mean to be distracting. They were all wondering: *Can she make all three?*

I shot.

Swish!

"Swiiiiiiiish!"

Kyle in the pep band starting pounding on his drum. I saw my mom and dad jump to their feet. The ref's whistle blew, and I ran down the court, adrenaline racing through my veins.

Caroline had the ball, took a shot, and missed the basket. But it didn't matter. The buzzer blared. We had won by three points! Maybe we didn't need all those points, but I was sure glad that I had made them.

I wanted to scream with happiness or jump for joy, but first we congratulated the Mavericks. When it came time to slap hands with 17, I looked her in the eyes.

"You were awesome," I said, and she just nodded. For a second, I felt really bad for her. I knew what it was like to play my heart out, without being able to take home the win.

Then everyone on the team came together, crushing one another in a group hug.

"We did it!" Bianca said.

"Everyone played amazing!" I added.

Coach Ramirez was grinning harder than I'd ever seen her. "Great job, Nighthawks. Playoffs, here we come!"

What's Next?

appy! Basketball! I formed into Beth's hand.
Beth smiled at me. *Happy!* she formed
back.

It had been such a crazy day! After the game,
everybody had gone out to celebrate: the team, the
boosters, and Blake and the basketball boys. We got
really loud and ate a million hamburgers and most
of us promised that we would try to get to the boys'
game later that night.

That meant I had a few hours of free time, and I
knew I'd been ignoring two very important members

of my family: Beth and Zobe. So when I got home, I hung out with Beth for a while. Then I decided to take Zobe for a walk while it was still light out.

It was chilly, so I put on a puffy vest, a beanie, and slipped on some gloves. I could see my breath as I walked down the street toward the park.

"How are you doing, Zobe? Do I need to buy you a sweater?" I asked him, but he looked pretty happy as he trotted alongside me toward Greenmont Park.

Because it was cold, only a few people dotted the walking trail that circled the park. I could make out a girl, and a dog with droopy ears inside the fenced-in dog park across the field. My heart jumped a little when I realized who it was.

"Amanda!" I called out, and Zobe and I jogged across the field. She looked up and smiled at me.

"Thanks for that pass today," she said when I reached her.

"You're the one who got open," I said. "Those Maverick girls were hard to shake."

She nodded. "No kidding!"

I opened the gate and walked inside with Zobe. I

took him off his leash and he trotted up to Freckles. They sniffed each other and then took off running.

"Just thought I'd take Freckles before I head out to the boys' game," Amanda said. Then she shivered. "*Brrr!* It's cold out."

"I'm going too," I said, and then there was a short, awkward silence between us. It was the first time we'd been alone since Friday night at the volley-ball game. I wasn't going to let her get away without finishing the conversation this time.

"So, you know, the other night . . ." My voice trailed off, but I found my courage. "You said things between us were complicated. What did you mean?"

Amanda looked at me, and I couldn't help noticing how green her eyes were. Not watery green, like some people's eyes, but bright green, like jewels or something.

"I'm sorry, it's just me being weird," she said. "I guess I just got really confused about our friendship after you left the basketball team. Even before that . . . we keep trying to make plans together, but we only really hang out when we walk our dogs."

I nodded. "Yeah, I'm sorry. I've been having a problem fitting in everything I want to do. Even Avery was really mad at me."

"I know you're busy," Amanda said. "And I understand. I was really happy when you came back to the team, but I miss playing center. Coach doesn't put me in as much anymore."

I didn't know what to say to that. I knew how much it stunk to be kept on the bench when you wanted to play. I nodded, not sure what to say.

Amanda threw up her hands. "That's silly, I know it! If I want to play more, I need to practice more. That's why I said it's complicated. Plus, the season will be over soon. Then what happens? Will we even be friends? Or will I go back to hanging out with the band kids while you hang out with the sports girls?"

"Of course we'll be friends," I said. And then I blurted out, "I like you, Amanda."

I felt my face get hot. Why? Why was me liking Amanda any different than the way I liked Avery or Blake or Dylan?

"I like you, too," Amanda said, and a blush spread across her freckled cheeks.

What was this feeling I was having? Was it a crush? I'd never had one before, so I wasn't sure what that should feel like. Was this how Blake felt when he was around Bianca? I'd have to ask him—or wait, that would be too awkward!

I had the strange urge to just run right home. Then Zobe ran up to me and nearly knocked me over. Amanda and I both laughed.

I suddenly felt something cold on my cheek and looked up. "Hey, it's snowing!" I said.

Amanda stuck out her tongue and caught a snowflake. "Icy!"

"Is it supposed to snow a lot?" I wondered. "I hope we can get to the boys' game."

She checked her phone. "Just flurries. It should be good. Do you want a ride?"

I nodded. "Yeah, I'm sure my dad could use a break."

We leashed our dogs and walked out of the park

together as the snow fell around us. Zobe started to do a happy dog dance.

"Look! He loves the snow!" I said.

Amanda laughed. "Snow doggy!"

We both stopped in front of Amanda's house.

"I'll text you before we pick you up," she said.

"Great," I said, and I almost turned to go, but I hesitated. "Amanda, I promise we'll still be friends after the basketball season ends."

She grinned. "Good."

"But the season's not over yet," I reminded her. "We still have to win the playoffs!"

"Go, Nighthawks!" she said, and then she walked inside her house.

I smiled. Just a few months ago, I had been pretty miserable even though I had an awesome family and two amazing best friends. I was upset that I wasn't playing shooting guard. Freaked out about wearing a fancy dress to the dance. And not sure if I even loved playing basketball.

Now I knew that I loved playing basketball, and

being center. I had a new friend, Amanda. I still had my awesome family and my amazing best friends. And I also had the best dog in the world, a dog who was just as big and as goofy as I was, a dog who helped me learn to love myself as much as I loved him.

So much had changed in just those few months! I had no idea what the next few months would bring, but I had a feeling, deep down, that there would always be good things along with the bad.

"Come on, Zobe!" I said, and he picked up his pace. We jogged home, dodging snowflakes as we ran.